EVIL IN MY TOWN

Karen Ann Hopkins

ISBN: 978-1-097-85017-4 (paperback)
ISBN 13: 978-0-578-51252-5 (ebook)

Books by Karen Ann Hopkins

Serenity's Plain Secrets
in reading order
LAMB TO THE SLAUGHTER
WHISPERS FROM THE DEAD
SECRETS IN THE GRAVE
HIDDEN IN PLAIN SIGHT
PAPER ROSES
EVIL IN MY TOWN
FORBIDDEN WAYS (a romantic companion novel)

Wings of War
in reading order
EMBERS
GAIA
TEMPEST
ETERNITY

The Temptation Novels
in reading order
TEMPTATION
BELONGING
FOREVER
DECEPTION

For you, Mom. Thanks for being my biggest fan, and the person I can turn to with my problems and my accomplishments. I love you!

ACKNOWLEDGMENTS

Many thanks go out to Grace Bell Morris for putting her heart and soul into the edits, and to Heather Miller for her focused proofreading skills. A huge shout out to Jenny Zemanek of Seedlings Design for another amazing cover.

As always, much appreciation and love to my husband, Jay, and five children, Luke, Cole, Lily, Owen, and Cora, for all the everyday little things and support to make this crazy dream possible.

1

December 2nd
Blood Rock, Indiana

The straps of the backpack dug into Jackson Merritt's shoulders. The discomfort was welcomed. It kept him focused as he walked through the front doors of the Blood Rock Public High School with the crowded stream of other teenagers. The hissing noise of the bus door opening disappeared behind him, swallowed by the mingling of voices, laughter, and sharp calls between students.

Jackson's eyes shifted to the security guard standing outside the school's office. Mr. Dodgly grimaced when Miss Forester, one of the science teachers, said something to him. The guard wasn't paying any attention to the kids entering the building, except to pause when a few of the football players began swatting each other, stalling everyone's forward movement.

"Get moving, Ricks, Bruins, and Binotti," Mr. Dodgly shouted, gesturing them onward.

A couple of the athletes waved back at the security guard, yelling out greetings. The crowd parted around the noisy group, mostly ignoring them, except for a couple of girls who hooted encouragement to the smaller player who was still scuffling with Bruins.

Jackson jerked his head, licking his lips and forcing away the frown from his face. It was the same every day. The teenagers of Blood Rock High School were incredibly predictable. The same kids, doing the same things—every day. Mr. Dodgly, the teachers, and the office personnel lived in a delusional world, where the worst thing they imagined might happen on any given day was a hallway fight or drugs turning up in a locker. Most of the adults only paid attention to the pretty girls, star players, and brainy kids. Jackson didn't fit into any of those categories, so he slipped under the radar. His grades were okay, he wasn't on a team, and with his average height and plain face, he didn't stand out in any particular way.

Principle Evergreen poked her head out from her office door. Their eyes briefly met. Her quick gaze passed right over Jackson without any recognition. She disappeared again and Jackson exhaled. He hadn't realized he'd been holding his breath.

When he raised his head, the black hands on the wall clock jumped out at him with booming sharpness. Seven forty-five. He swallowed hard as his heart banged against his rib cage.

So far it had been easy. *Way too easy,* he thought.

The first bell rang and everyone surged forward. A freshman girl bumped into him. She was wearing glasses and her hair was pulled up in a ponytail.

"Sorry!" she chirped, flashing him a smile before she turned away.

Jackson's eyes widened. Within a minute the hallway would be empty. His head swiveled and he scanned the crowd.

Even though the students were hustling to get to their

homerooms, they appeared to be moving in slow motion to Jackson. His heart throbbed into his throat. Sweat broke out on his forehead, and at the nape of his neck, just beneath his scruffy, sandy colored hair.

A boy planted a kiss on his girlfriend's lips before she entered a classroom. Three more girls huddled outside the bathroom. The football players finally caught up and jogged by, creating a path that others followed.

It was that moment when Jackson found who he was looking for. The scene in the hallway blurred. He unzipped and dropped his backpack in a single motion. His hands closed around the cool aluminum, and with a deft movement, he slid the pin that connected the upper receiver and barrel to the stock.

When Jackson raised the AR-15, his vision cleared and he began shooting.

2

SERENITY

I tugged the material up over my breasts, sucking in my breath.

"Dammit. It's squishing my boobs," I growled.

"Do you need help?" CJ's voice was perky, and I did my best to force a smile on my face. At least she was enjoying herself.

I nudged the door open and she slipped into the large mint green dressing room.

"Oh, it's beautiful," she gushed. "Once I get you zipped up, you'll see what I mean."

"But it's too tight," I complained.

She worked the zipper up and spun me around. As I stared at my reflection, she rambled on.

"It has a built-in corset, Serenity. It's supposed to feel snug. That dress gives you a figure like a Grecian statue."

"That's a good thing?" I stared hard at my reflection in the mirror. The ivory material was delicately laced around the bodice, exposing the cleavage that the corset created. Folds of material flared out, falling to the floor around me like something a princess in a faraway kingdom would wear. "I look ridiculous."

"It's very fashionable and it's perfect on your slim figure," CJ replied. Her head tilted as she eyed me up and down. Her voice had lost its excitement when she went on to say, "Well, maybe it isn't you after all. The most important thing about a wedding dress is that you feel beautiful in it."

"And comfortable," I added. My eyes drifted back to the gown hanging on the peg. It was a short-sleeved sheath dress I'd tried on earlier. It was detailed with just the right amount of lace, and it didn't have a torture contraption inside it to make my boobs two cup sizes larger. I was trim and fit—I needed to be for my job. My entire wardrobe was all about freedom of movement so I could chase, and hopefully catch the bad guys. "How do you know so much about wedding dresses anyway?" I dared to lift my eyes in her direction.

CJ shrugged, and her brown curls bounced on her shoulders when she chuckled. "I've been a bridesmaid in eight weddings." My jaw dropped as she counted on her fingers, whispering to herself. "This makes nine all together."

"That's incredible. I haven't had nine girlfriends in my entire lifetime," I puffed the words out as I tried to cover the awe in my voice.

She laughed. "The funny thing is I don't even speak to any of those girls anymore." She pursed her lips, becoming thoughtful. "They just wanted large wedding parties, and I was always available."

I gripped CJ's arm, giving her a little shake. "You're one of the nicest women I know. I'm sure when those brides-to-be asked you to be in their weddings, they did it because you're fun, kind, and responsible. They knew you'd actually show up and do everything you were supposed to do." The melancholy look had settled on her face, and her green eyes had become dull. I quickly added, "They knew you'd make their wedding party pictures prettier." I squeezed her shoulders before dropping my hands.

A polite smile was fixated on her face. "If you say so… It's just that as I've gotten older, I've realized how most of the people I used to think I was so close to, I really wasn't. When I broke up with Ryan, none of those *friends* even contacted me to see how I was doing. To make matters even worse, since their new hubbies were buddies with my ex, they simply moved onto friendships with his new girlfriend, forgetting about me all together." One of her brows rose. "You know how cops are."

I managed a wavering smile, searching my memories for something I could say. Todd Roftin, my first deputy, had annoyed me since middle school, but when we became partners, we became family. And that meant that his wife, Heather, became my friend, too.

"As you get older your friend group is supposed to get smaller, I think," I offered. I couldn't really recall having such a domestic conversation in a long time. Being Blood Rock's Sheriff meant I was usually too busy investigating crimes to give much thought to normal things. I was a bit out of my element here, but I could see that CJ needed something more from me, or she wouldn't have brought up the whole friends-not-being-friends subject. "I can count on two hands the people I trust in this world—and you're among that elite group, CJ. Quality is far better than quantity if you ask me."

CJ smiled. "Friendship to you is about loyalty, isn't it?"

"Of course. If someone doesn't have your back, what good are they?"

"Are you sure Daniel has your back?" CJ asked. Her tone was not accusatory, just curious.

I pictured my fiancé. He was tall, muscled, and gorgeous. His wavy dark brown hair was unruly and his brown eyes were always dark with passion. He was serious and laidback at the same time. He was the best lover I had ever had, and he always had my back. But he used to be Amish, and that one thing had kept me from committing to him for a while. He thought differently than I did about a lot of things—like faith and forgiveness. He saw the good in people. Whereas I usually saw the bad, and for good reason. In my line of work, I spent too much time dealing with the darker side of human nature. I'd seen true evil up close and personal. I was definitely jaded from my experiences.

"Do you all need some help in there? I'd be happy to pull some more dresses from the sales floor for you," the saleslady said with a cheerful voice outside the door.

"No, we're finishing up here," I called out and then met CJ's questioning gaze. "I'm not really worried about Daniel. I'm the one with the issues in our relationship." I leaned back against the wall. "I don't know if I have what it takes to be a regular wife—"

"Regular?" CJ interrupted.

"You know, make dinner, clean the house, that sort of stuff."

"But you already live together, so he must have low expectations for those things." She grinned.

I drew in a deep breath. "I don't think I want kids, CJ."

She leaned back. "Haven't you talked to him about that subject yet?"

I scrunched up my face. "Yes, I've said as much to him, but Daniel is an optimist. He probably believes I'll change my mind eventually."

"He wants children?"

"Sure. He's ex-Amish. Having kids comes naturally in the culture he grew up in. Hell, if he doesn't have at least four or five, he'll be out of his element." I shook my head, trying to imagine myself being the mother of even one child, much less a whole passel.

"Just because he was Amish doesn't mean he wants to have a ton on kids. Look at Joshua. He only has three kids." CJ sounded weary.

I crossed my arms, hardening my expression. "How is Joshua Miller?" I asked, changing the uncomfortable subject.

"The same as far as I know. I haven't seen him since I moved into the apartment a month ago. I still don't know what I'm going to do, either."

The creases at the corner of her eyes deepened and her eyes glistened. I felt like crap. "Sorry, it's none of my business. I shouldn't have asked."

"No, I understand." She cleared her throat. "We've been friends for a while, Serenity, but you also saved my life. I'll never forget how you rescued me from Caleb—" She shuddered.

I wagged a finger at her. "Let's not reminisce about that night. This is supposed to be a happy day."

Her head bobbed up and down. "I'm sorry! You're right. No more Debbie-downer." She snatched the slim, short sleeved gown from the peg. "So is this the one?"

I gazed at the dress again. I loved the simplicity of it, yet the small amount of lace and the delicate nature of the material made it pretty. "I wish Laura could have made it today."

I chewed my bottom lip, thinking about my sister and her marital problems. The fact that she and her husband were at a counseling session was beyond disturbing. I hadn't even known they were having problems until recently.

"This one really is you, Serenity," CJ said softly. I met her gaze. We were both in the same boat—feeling a little out of sorts and lonely lately.

I took the dress from her and draped it over my arm. "I'm not a gown type of gal, but if I have to wear one, this dress feels the best."

The shadow of sadness disappeared from CJ's face. "Yes!" She scrolled something on a piece of paper and held it up. *I said yes to the dress.*

"I guess I did." I returned the gown to the peg. "Unzip this thing so I can breathe again," I ordered.

I turned, and just as CJ's fingers reached the zipper, my buzzer went off at the same time that my phone rang. My chest tightened like it always did when a call came in simultaneously on both devices. It usually meant big trouble.

CJ grabbed my tote bag and handed it to me. My cellphone lit up again, vibrating, and it was joined by the blaring sound of the emergency tone from CJ's phone. She pulled her phone from her pocket and gasped.

"What the hell"—I scanned the emergency alert—"oh my God. There's an active shooter at the high school."

3

TAYLOR

op. Pop. Pop. Pop. Pop. Pop. Pop. Pop. Pop…
My ears were ringing and my legs turned to jelly. Everyone began running and screaming. Crystal dropped. A second earlier she'd been walking alongside me, babbling about her annoying weekend spent at her father's. Dillon went down ahead of me. I had to jump to avoid stepping on what was left of his bloodied head.

Pop. Pop. Pop. Pop. Pop. Pop.
Tessa screamed, falling to the floor.
Someone smashed into my back and I stumbled forward. Before I could catch my balance, someone else shoved me aside and I slammed into a locker.

Pop. Pop. Pop. Pop. Pop. Pop. Pop. Pop.
Ms. Fletcher was on the floor. The front of her blouse was torn and covered with blood. She clutched little Jimmy Cramer in her arms. His head lolled to the side and his dead eyes stared.

Pop. Pop. Pop. Pop. Pop. Pop. Pop.

Someone wailed, another yelped.

Mr. Dodgly or maybe another teacher shouted orders, "Run! Get up! Move."

I had been unconsciously counting in my numb mind. Thirty rounds. He's out.

I didn't look back. My neck was stiff and my heart pounded so hard I thought it would explode into my throat. I couldn't say anything. My throat burned.

Move, I ordered myself. My legs came to life and I stepped around Ms. Fletcher, who wasn't moving at all.

Snap. Snap. Schick...

The little sounds behind me were familiar. They roared in my head and made my skin crawl. I never liked guns, but my aunt was the sheriff in town. Going to the shooting range was Aunt Reni's idea of bonding time with her teenage niece.

A science classroom was ahead on the left. I stretched out my legs and ran. The bodies became fuzzy as I dodged them, jagging right and then left.

I had almost reached the doorway when a hand rose up and swiped at my leg. Shivering with shock, I squatted and grabbed for my friend Lindsey. The blonde hair on the side of her head was a bloody mess. She whimpered, "Help me."

"We have to go." I tugged her limp body up. "Move, Lindsey! Get up!"

Lindsey wrapped her arm around mine, and I hoisted her upwards with strength that wasn't my own.

Her muffled cries were in my ear as we hobbled to the door that was now closed. My hand gripped the handle and turned, but it didn't move. I banged my fist into the wood.

"Let us in! He's reloading. Please—we'll die!"

I chanced a glance over my shoulder. There were bodies everywhere. Some were piled together, others were alone, contorted in unnatural positions. But it was the shooter who had my attention.

My stomach reeled as recognition lit my mind. *Jackson Merritt.* His dispassionate, shark eyes met mine and fear screamed in my head.

Jackson raised the rifle. A sickening smirk twisted his lips.

"Please, please open the door," I begged. Lindsey slumped into me, her body rocking with gasps.

Pop.

The doorframe next to my head splintered. I recoiled and found myself falling backward with Lindsey. Hands came from out of nowhere. My shoulders were roughly grabbed and I was dragged across the threshold.

The door slammed shut. *Pop.* The next round hit the door with an explosion, but it didn't penetrate the wood.

"Come on. We have to get out of here," a voice urged.

I blinked. The classroom was empty. Backpacks and books were thrown about on the tables and desks. A boy disappeared through a doorway at the back of the room. He was moving so fast I wasn't sure who it was, but the person whose hands pulled me to my feet I did know. *Hunter Pollard.*

Raspy breaths scraped my throat. "It's Jackson—he's killing everyone."

Pop. Pop. Pop. Pop.

"That's why we have to go. Now, Taylor." Hunter pulled on my arm.

I jerked him to a stop. "What about Lindsey?" She was crumpled on the floor.

He shook his head. "I think she's dead or dying. We can't help her."

I looked up. Hunter's blue eyes were wide with terror. The only reason he had been able to pull the two of us inside the room so quickly was because he was unusually tall and well built for a teenager. He attributed it to all the work he did on his family's farm, but knowing his parents, I would say it had as much to do with good genes as throwing hay bales.

Something thudded against the hallway door that led to the apocalyptic scene. The sound made the knot in my throat leap upwards. I glanced back at Lindsey's prone form one last time and let Hunter drag me across the room and through the back doorway. The smaller hallway was dimly lit and long. It led to the far side of the gymnasium and the agricultural classrooms.

Pop. Pop. Pop. Pop. Pop.

The blasts were getting closer. My eyes burned when I thought of Lindsey. Had Jackson just shot her again?

Hunter grabbed a door handle, but it wouldn't lift. "Locked." He tugged me to the next door. The same thing happened, and he cussed, kicking it before we took off again.

Pop.

The bullet thrummed past my head, striking the wall. I glanced over my shoulder. Jackson walked into the small hallway and held the semi-automatic rifle confidently at his chest.

"Why are you doing this?" I choked out the words.

Hunter gripped my hand tighter and we turned into another hallway. It was even smaller and darker than the last one. I couldn't recall ever having been here before.

Jackson's voice sounded far away. "You know why!"

A shiver shot up my spine and sliced into my head.

"No… no…no," I mumbled through the wetness of the tears streaking down my face.

A door finally opened for Hunter, and we fell into the darkness. I bumped into something wooden and Hunter whispered, "It's a storeroom for the theater club."

"I can't see." I panicked, swiping the air in front of me.

"Shhh, we can't turn on the lights. Trust me. There's a place to hide back here."

My terror was interrupted for a moment, wondering how Hunter knew anything about the theater's storage area. I stubbed my foot and pressed my hand to my mouth to keep from crying out.

Pop. Pop. Pop. Jackson was getting closer.

I pushed against Hunter's back. I didn't like being trapped in an unfamiliar place, and I certainly wasn't comfortable about trusting him. He was trouble—and today's horror proved it.

"Almost there," he coaxed from the darkness.

Our hands were sweaty, and mine almost slid out of his when he sped up. Hunter pulled up and then disappeared in the inky blackness.

"Where are you?" I whispered fervently.

There was silence and another *pop* sounded just beyond the door.

My heart pounded too loudly. Jackson might even hear it if he stepped into to the storage room. I sucked in a shaky breath.

"Here, give me your hand and climb up." I saw the dim outline of Hunter's hand only a few feet away.

I thrust my hands upward. When my fingers found his, I let out a quick gasp of relief. He guided me up narrow steps and along what I imagined was a wide plank supported by brackets of some kind. There was a creaking sound and he lifted me over a short wall and into a wooden box. The space was so small that when I dropped to my knees I was forced to press tightly against Hunter.

Just as he lowered the lid, the room lit up.

"He's here," Hunter muttered into my ear.

The only thing that gave me hope was the muffled sound of sirens in the distance. Aunt Reni was coming.

But would she make it in time to save us?

4

SERENITY

My 9mm was in my hands as I sprinted into the school with over a dozen other officers from several departments. The building was at the edge of town, making the three minute trip excruciating. There was no time to brief the officers or devise a plan. Kids were dying in the school, and the best chance we had to stop the devastation was to rush the building with our own guns blazing.

I motioned for half of the group to turn left when we entered the front door and the rest came with me. We'd trained for this horrifying possibility, but nothing could have prepared us for what we encountered when we entered the south hallway.

"My God!" Todd exclaimed. Deputy Jeremy Dickens lurched forward, kneeling beside a red headed girl who was curled up in a ball, crying.

"Dickens, you fall back and help these kids and teachers until the EMTs arrive," I ordered.

I lifted my chin. Todd and the others followed. "Clear this

hallway and check the rooms," I instructed Hernandez, Scott, and Baker. "We have to get the EMTs in here." They nodded and dropped back.

It was hard to step over bodies with just a glance and barely a pause, but I knew how large and mazelike the building was. The shooter was still at large and students were trapped and hiding. I couldn't help the kids who were already dead. The ones with traumatic injuries would be taken care of by Beth, Raymond, and the other emergency responders who were arriving at the scene. But I could stop the son of a bitch who did this. That was my goal: to save the living and to find my niece.

My calm outward demeanor belied the rapid beating of my heart. Years of handling emergency situations, including a mass shooting at a wedding, gave me the experience to remain steady. At this moment there was no decorum. We had stepped back into a time where the good citizens had to take up arms and shoot back at the evil ones, just like in an old western movie.

"How could this happen in our school, Serenity," Todd muttered.

I risked a glance his way. His hands were firm on his gun and his eyes darted around. He was my best sharp shooter. I understood his shock and pain. I felt it too. We had walked these same halls when we were teens, and now, besides my sixteen-year-old niece being in danger, Todd had twin nephews who were freshmen this year. I knew what he feared most.

"Get a hold of yourself. We need all our wits to save them," I said in a low voice.

My quick gaze eliminated my niece, Taylor, or Todd's nephews from the victims on the ground ahead of us. I had counted eighteen down so far. Most weren't moving at all, but a few were keening or moaning, rocking their heads back and forth. I heard the officers quietly speaking to the injured. They would reach the suffering victims on this end very soon. I only prayed that it was quick enough for some of the more gravely wounded.

As per protocol, the classroom doors were closed, so I sped up into a jog when I spotted one that was flung open. It was a science room, and the damage to the wooden frame and door was unmistakable. The killer had picked this door to break into for some reason, and my gut told me he had gone through it.

I looked back at Todd and he nodded. He was ready, even anxious to enter the room.

I took a fervent breath and peeked in, scanning the interior. There was a female victim on the floor, but otherwise the room was empty.

I recognized Taylor's friend and my heart plummeted into my stomach. The girls were always together. Lindsey's mom was one of our town's social workers. I hurried to her side and felt for a pulse. She moaned and I blew out in relief. The bullet appeared to have grazed the side of her head—she might survive.

Todd knelt beside me. "Is this Sherry's daughter?"

I nodded. "Stay with her until the medical team arrives. Sherry wouldn't want her to be conscious and alone for even a minute."

Todd grasped my arm as I rose. "Be alert. I'll catch up as soon as I can."

I met his gaze and then pulled away. I crossed the room to the back door and carefully looked down the narrow hallway.

The floor was clear of bodies, but there were cratered bullet holes in the wall. The killer had taken aim, but missed. Or he was shooting rounds off to intimidate. I followed the damaged places on the walls, not bothering with the few closed doorways I passed. The killer had moved quickly down this hallway, and my guess was he was following someone.

The gymnasium doors were directly ahead, but I paused at the hallway that jutted off to the right. I knew from experience that this hallway led to the janitor's equipment room and the drama club's storage room. The hallway was dimly lit and always quiet. I stepped lightly, listening as I moved sideways, keeping my back to the wall. Fourteen years earlier, I'd snuck down this exact same hall, holding Denton's hand and giggling all the way to the private storage rooms where we'd steal a few kisses before the morning bell rang. I never dreamed I'd be retracing my steps years later in pursuit of a school shooter.

I passed another bullet hole that was about even with my head, and moved with the precision and purpose of a heat-seeking missile when I spied the light spilling into the hallway. I remembered it to be where the theater production sets were kept.

I strained to hear something, but all was quiet except for the wailing sirens beyond the school's walls, and the random shouts from officers and emergency personnel in the distance. The first responders would be clearing the school, room by room, hallway by hallway. Their main objectives were to evacuate the wounded and everyone else out of the school and away from danger as quickly as possible. We'd learned from past mass shootings that the best approach was to rush the building and save whoever we could. Interrupting the shooter usually put him on the run, saving lives immediately. The calls we received from the school reported only one active shooter, but as I covered the distance to the storage room, I kept an eye out for any surprise appearances from either direction.

I stayed in the shadow when I reached the doorway. The sound of shuffled movement and then a knock made me stop. I lifted my gun and licked my lips before I rounded the door. Boxes were piled high and racks full of colorful costumes lined the side walls. The back of the large open room had scaffolding to store the larger set props. There was a neatly piled stack of lumber and some carpenter tools strewn across a wooden table. I took several steps to reach the closest rack.

Once I had some cover, I made a decision. Someone was hiding in here, but whether it was a scared kid or the shooter was the question. My instinct told me the killer was close by, so I took a gamble. "This is Sheriff Adams. Come out with your hands up and you won't get hurt."

I thought I heard chuckling, but the sound abruptly ended. Following the noise, I moved against the costumes, trying to stay hidden. "Time is running out. Show yourself."

There was a thud and a box crashed to the floor.

I spun on my heel, my gun raised. Someone was behind those boxes. I tried to calm my beating heart with a deep breath. I was painfully aware of my finger resting on the trigger guard. I didn't want to make a mistake.

A vision rose up in my mind of another time and place.

Dim light from the lamp overhead sprayed down on the scene and the smell of the wet pavement filled my nostrils. My heart pounded furiously as I watched the gloved hand slip into the opening of the oversized coat with the Colts logo in the upper left-hand corner.

"Keep your hands where I can see them! Raise your fucking hands!" I shouted.

My voice pounded in my ears, matching the beating of my heart. I held my gun steadily and became intensely calm. Refusing to obey me, the individual's hand went deeper into the coat, pulling something shiny out. Their body tilted toward my partner, Ryan, just before I pulled the trigger.

It was a teenage girl I'd shot and killed that day. She'd been an accomplice to the killing of an elderly woman, but she didn't have to die. I often wondered what I could have done differently, how I could have saved that girl instead of killing her. This scenario was very different. The sick kid who'd just killed dozens of his classmates didn't deserve leniency, but I wouldn't take the chance of shooting an innocent victim, either. I had to be restrained and yet, ready to act.

"Come out with your hands up! Show yourself!" I ordered, stepping out into the open. My gaze was fixated on the stack of boxes.

The sounds of the officers shouting, "Clear," were getting closer. Backup was on the way.

I took another step. "Come on out. It's over."

"Aunt Reni, watch out!"

Her voice echoed in my ears as I turned and looked up. The lid of a wood crate was lifted, and I could just make out Taylor's big blue eyes and blonde hair—but there was someone else on the scaffolding with her. The shooter wore a grey sweat suit and held an AR-15 in his hands. I could see the acne on his cheeks. He was just a kid.

His attention snapped from me to the box where my niece was hiding. He swiveled and aimed at the box.

I pulled the trigger and he folded. There were two *pop-pops* from his weapon. The kid's body struck the side of the plank and tumbled sideways over the edge. He hit the floor with a sickening crunch.

"Stay where you are, Taylor," I shouted.

I kicked the rifle away and dropped down beside the killer. I didn't need to check for a pulse. His neck was bent in a grotesque way, twisting too far back.

"You got our guy?" Todd called out from the doorway.

I rocked back on my heels and looked over my shoulder. Todd entered the room with Dickens, Hernandez, and Baker. Their guns were drawn.

"Lower your weapons. We've got him," I said.

Todd reached me first. He stared down at the body. "Damn, Serenity."

"I shot his thigh. It was the fall that killed him." I raised my head at the crying noises. Taylor was standing beside a guy I didn't recognize. He had his arms around her as she shook against him with her soft sobs. "Come on down, kids. It's safe now." I nodded to Jeremy. "Go on and assist them down those steps."

"Sure thing, boss." Jeremy hurried to the ladder.

I finally looked at Todd. His eyes were moist and beads of sweat dotted his forehead. "What's your estimation of fatalities?"

Todd rubbed the side of his temple. "It's bad. Really bad. Twenty-five to thirty."

The adrenaline coursing through my veins kept my mind clear and my voice fixed. "Is Lindsey going to make it?"

"When I left, Beth was loading her onto a gurney. The girl was conscious, but I don't know any more than that."

When Taylor's feet touched the floor I went to her and

caught her up in my arms. For the first time since the call came in at the bridal shop, I sagged a little. "It's okay—it's over." I smoothed her hair back from her face. At least my sister would get good news today, but so many others would not.

I didn't even try to wipe the tears that began to trail down my cheeks.

5

TAYLOR

I wiggled out of Mom's overly tight embrace and turned to face Aunt Reni. I blinked at the bright lights in the lobby of the sheriff's department and rubbed my arms for warmth.

"Is it necessary to interview her right now? She's been through so much already." Disapproval flickered in Mom's eyes. Her voice shook. "Her best friend is in critical condition and she knew most of the victims."

I glanced at Aunt Reni. She wasn't in her usual uniform. Her faded blue jeans and light blue sweater were in stark contrast with the serious look on her face.

"I'm sorry, Laura. I want to talk to Taylor while the events are still fresh in her mind."

Mom took a step forward and leaned in toward her sister. "I'm not happy about this. Taylor should be home resting, not being interrogated. The shooter is dead. What more can she add to the story at this moment that's going to make any difference at all?"

Aunt Reni's eyes narrowed. "I'm not asking, Laura, I'm insisting."

I held my breath and stared at Mom. Her cheeks reddened and her eyes widened. She was five years older than Aunt Reni. They both had the same blond hair and slight figures, but Mom had more lines on her face and her hair was shorter.

Silence hung in the air between the two women even though the lobby was full of officers, parents, and teachers. Some people were crying, others were moving quietly about. The look of shock shone clearly on everyone's faces. It still seemed unreal. Twenty-three kids and three teachers were dead, and Lindsey was in bad shape. She might die too. I rubbed my eyes again, wiping the tears around my wet face.

"A few minutes and that's all," Mom snapped.

Aunt Reni motioned for me to follow her into her office, but put her hand up when Mom tried to follow. "Since I'm her aunt, it's all right for me to do a quick, informal interview. I'd like you to wait outside."

My head swiveled back to Mom. Her face had paled and her brow knitted. The clash between them was surprising. They usually got along pretty well, but things had changed a little since Mom and Dad had started talking about divorce. The idea seemed to bother Aunt Reni almost as much as it upset my brother, Will, and myself.

In one more act of submission, Mom backed down and went back out into the lobby.

Aunt Reni shut the door behind me, squeezed my shoulder, and directed me to one of the two chairs on the side of the desk opposite her. She took the seat behind the desk, sat forward and folded her arms in front of her. I gazed out the window. The clouds were thick and cold grayness clung to the trees. It looked like it might snow.

"Are you all right?" Aunt Reni's voice was softer than the tone she'd used with Mom. I hated the sound of her pity. It just made me want to begin crying all over again.

"I'm tired." I forced myself to look directly at my aunt and swallowed the knot down my throat. "But I'm a lot better off than all those kids and teachers. They're dead, Aunt Reni."

"I know. It's terrible what happened in the school today. If there was any way I could have prevented it from happening, I would have, but it's over. Now, we bury our dead and try to move on the best we can."

"That's awfully cold of you," I challenged, raising my chin.

Aunt Reni leaned back and glanced out the window. I wondered if the icy, wicked looking day affected her as much as it did me. A shiver passed through me and I stuck my hands in the deep pockets of my jacket. The frozen image of a bloody Ms. Fletcher holding Jimmy Cramer in her arms appeared in my mind. They were both among the dead.

I sucked in a breath and trembled. Aunt Reni raced around the desk and knelt before me. She placed her hands on my knees. "It's okay for you to grieve, Taylor. You can cry or scream, whatever you need to do. The memories are never going away." She must have seen the look of horror on my face, because she hurriedly added, "But they diminish over time. You see, you shouldn't completely forget what happened anyway. Evil was unleashed and innocent people died. We can't bring them back, but it's my job to find closure for the victims' families. In order for them to have peace"—she spoke forcefully—"for me to have peace, I have to figure out why Jackson Merritt stole his older brother's AR-15, took it apart and hid it in his backpack to ultimately open fire on his classmates and teachers." She rose and walked back around her desk. "I have to know why he did such a thing. What set him off? What or who pushed him over the edge? Was he a ticking time bomb that every person of authority in his life missed seeing, or did something else happen to the kid that made him commit such evil and ultimately cost him his own life?"

I sniffed and nodded slowly.

"Don't you want to understand why Jackson Merritt killed your classmates?"

I found my voice. "Yes, of course."

Aunt Reni sat down and stared at me. "Good. That's the first step in healing, Taylor. I've seen more horrible things than you can imagine, but what keeps me sane is the ability to do something to help the people who are suffering most when crimes are committed. Justice helps healing. Knowing the truth also makes it easier to get up and go on after something like this happens. Truth is power. And that's what I need your help with—discovering the truth."

"Maybe it's completely random and there aren't any answers," I said.

"I used to think that, but over the years and after dozens of homicide investigations, I've learned that there's always an answer. It might not make any sense to reasonable, good people—but there's answers that help us understand even the most horrific crimes." She snorted. "The answers never give justification for a mass tragedy like this, but they help us heal. Perhaps even force changes that will help us identify troubled individuals like Jackson, and prevent shootings like this in the future."

I sat up straighter. Aunt Reni's words made me feel

stronger, almost as if I actually could make things better, even if only in a small way. "What do you need from me?"

Aunt Reni pressed her fingers to her lips and narrowed her gaze on me. My heartrate sped up, but I didn't look away.

She picked up a pencil and scribbled something on the notebook in front of her. "Why were you hiding with Hunter Pollard?"

The question took me off guard. "He opened the door for me and Lindsey to escape into the classroom. If he hadn't pulled us in, we would have been gunned down for sure."

"Are you friends with Hunter?"

My palms began to sweat and I felt a little dizzy. Did Aunt Reni know something about Hunter? I shrugged. "Just around school, that's all." I tried to keep my voice from cracking.

Aunt Reni stared at me for several long breaths. "Were you friends with Jackson Merritt?"

"No," I quickly answered.

Her brows rose. "You never hung out with him or talked to him at school, or out of school?"

"No, no. Why are you asking me that?" I tilted my head, heat burning my face.

Aunt Reni tapped her pencil on the table and looked out the window again. When her gaze settled back on me, my stomach twisted into knots. "Jackson Merritt entered the Blood Rock High School at seven-forty this morning. He pulled out his weapon and began firing right after the first bell rang at seven forty-five. It appears that he shot people randomly at that point, probably trying to exact as much destruction as possible while the hallway was still crowded. When his thirty round magazine was empty, he went to reload." She took a long breath. "From what you and other witnesses have told me, and from our preliminary view of the crime scene, that's when you found Lindsey and went into the classroom with her." I nodded and she continued. "After Jackson reloaded, something changed. His focus pivoted from a desire to add as many bodies to the count as possible, to a hunting exhibition."

"Hunting?" The word tumbled from my mouth.

Aunt Reni pursed her lips. "He had a death wish, Taylor. There's a pretty good chance that if I hadn't shot him and he hadn't fallen to his death, he would have taken his own life. Yet, he left the more crowded area of the school to follow you and Hunter all the way down that vacant back hallway in a fairly methodical way." She leaned over the table and stared hard at me. "Was he after Hunter...or you?"

A memory flooded my senses. *The forest was dark and wet and my heart hammered in my chest. I didn't want to be there, but Lindsey had insisted. The campfire was almost out and the scent of wet coals wrinkled my nose. There was quiet laughter and Lindsey pushed me down into the folding chair. Hunter sat across the way. He was holding Danielle's hand, a sixteen-year-old foster kid I barely knew. The girl held a can of beer and her eyes were glazed and staring.*

Lindsey giggled and kissed Matthew's cheek. He whispered something in her ear.

There were two more people standing by the green pickup truck. I couldn't remember the one guy's face, only that he had messy dark hair that acted as a mask of sorts to hide his features. But the other guy I knew.

Jackson Merritt.

That memory stung my mind and the room began to spin, and then there was blackness.

6

SERENITY

"**S**he's lying." I rubbed my temples and looked up to see three pairs of eyes staring at me. "I know my niece very well. She's a good kid, not the type to seek out trouble, and she's honest to the core. She didn't want to lie to me, and she did a crappy job of it—but she was lying nonetheless. For a girl who never stops talking, she was unusually quiet about Jackson."

Daniel grunted. "Damn, Serenity. Look what Taylor went through today. She saw her classmates gunned down before her eyes, and then she was chased by the lunatic who did it. Maybe she's just too shell-shocked to speak much. Hell, she fainted. Why aren't you more sympathetic here?"

I leaned back and took a sharp breath, filling my lungs, before exhaling softly. Then, I took a gulp of the lukewarm black coffee. Bobby Humphrey, the town's coroner, was seated in one chair and Todd occupied the other. I'd finally managed to escape the mayor and the media after ten hours of interviews and discussions, in addition to my office's ongoing investigation.

Talking to the victims' families was the hardest part. They wanted to see their children, but there had been so many bodies and gore at the crime scene it had taken most of the day just to photograph and collect evidence before the dead could be bagged and removed from the school. I had to shake my head to clear the bloody images from my mind. If I focused too much on the fact that twenty-three of the fallen were just kids, I wouldn't have been able to do my job. The heartbreak would tear me apart.

It was inky dark outside and the window rattled from the hammering wind. A cold front was moving through and snow was forecasted by morning. I was able to breathe again, being in the quiet company of three of the men I trusted most in my life. Even so, I still couldn't shake the feeling of foreboding that jabbed at me.

When I met my fiancé's stare, I strained to remain patient. "I'm not being tough on Taylor. She passed out because she was thinking about something that overwhelmed her, and I'd bet my last dollar it had something to do with Jackson Merritt."

Todd spoke up. "What does it matter if your niece had contact with him at some point? He murdered twenty-six people. Taylor is lucky to be alive."

I pressed my lips together to gather my thoughts, but Bobby beat me to a response.

"Serenity has a gift. She's able to see the truth when it stares her in the face. Her instincts are, more often than not, dead on. We should hear her out. This might not be the simple tragedy we think it is," Bobby said.

"Tragedy? This is like the apocalypse for our little town. Besides the mountain of paperwork and slew of upcoming funerals, it seems like a fairly open and shut case. How could this get any worse?" Todd asked in a rising voice.

Bobby pushed his glasses up on his nose and offered me a curt nod to continue.

"It's not that I think there's any more danger, exactly. It's more of a…feeling that there's a lot more to Jackson's melt down than we realize," I said.

"What does your niece have to do with any of this?" Daniel asked.

"I don't know yet, but she isn't telling me the truth, and that scares the hell out of me." I leveled my gaze on each of the men in turn, before settling it back on Daniel. "Jackson went out of his way to target Taylor and Hunter, or one of them, and I want to find out why."

"Yeah, I get it. We need to understand why this kid cracked the way he did. Go easy on Taylor, Serenity. She's been through one hell of an ordeal," Daniel pressed.

There was a tapping on the door. "Come in," I called out.

Jeremy poked his head in. "I found out something you might be interested in, boss."

I waved him in and all eyes turned to the deputy.

Jeremy hated any kind of scrutiny, and he took a long breath before he spoke. "Do you remember that sixteen-year-old girl who was found in the park last summer—she over-dosed on heroin, laced with fentanyl?"

I searched my memories, recalling the girl with long, straight brown hair and hazel eyes. I'd never seen those eyes filled with life, though. They were glazed over and had stared back at me from the metal table in Bobby's examination room. She had been a pretty girl, with her entire life ahead of her, but like so many other young and old people alike these days, she'd thrown it all away to get a high that had killed her. I never forgot the kids I saw on the table.

"She was a foster kid, wasn't she?" I asked.

"Yes, that's the one," Jeremy confirmed.

"What of her?" My heart raced, imagining the connection before he responded.

"I thought you might be interested to know she was being fostered by Jackson Merritt's family when she ODed," Jeremy said quickly.

Daniel slumped against the wall and Bobby perked up. Todd shook his head.

I slapped my hand on the desk. "Well, boys, looks like there is more to this story after all..."

7

TAYLOR

L indsey's face was pale and her eyes were closed. Her hand was limp as I clasped it with my own.

"Thank you for coming, Taylor. When she wakes up, she'll be happy to see you," Lindsey's mom said.

I sniffed, fighting the tears that threatened to fall. "She will wake up, won't she?"

Mrs. Meade's eyes moistened. She hurriedly said, "Yes, dear, of course. The doctor said she's very lucky that the"— she stiffened, struggling with the word—"bullet only grazed her skull. It will be some time before she's back to her normal self, but she will get there again," she insisted, like she was trying to convince herself just as much as she was me.

I bobbed my head and Mrs. Meade put her arms around me, squeezing hard. "If you don't mind, I'm going to grab something to eat in the cafeteria. I haven't eaten all day."

I stepped back. "Go ahead. I'll stay with Lindsey."

"Do you want anything?"

"No, I'm fine. Thanks, though."

When Mrs. Meade was gone, I sat back down beside the hospital bed and stared at my friend. Tubes were running into her nose and her arm. The room was quiet except for the rhythmic pinging of the monitor connected to her. The sky beyond the window was dark and starless—like that night in the woods...

Lindsey was in the truck, making out with a guy who didn't even go to our school. Hunter was tugging on Danielle's hand, and Jackson sat on a log, watching the dying flames of the campfire.

"Dani, don't go back to the park. I'll take you home."

"It's a short walk." Danielle yawned. Her eyes were droopy and her words had come out slurred. From the pile of empty beer cans beside the fire, it was a pretty safe guess she was already drunk.

"I don't think that's a good idea, Danielle," I spoke up.

Danielle's head swiveled in my direction. "No one asked you. Why are you even here?"

I intertwining my fingers and avoided her fierce gaze.

"She came with her friend," Jackson said. "Just like me."

I glanced up and Jackson was looking at Danielle. The expression on his face made the hair go up on the back of my neck...

"Taylor?"

I blinked the memory away and leaned in closer to Lindsey. Her eyes were slits and her voice was weak, but she was awake.

"I'll get a nurse." I stood up. She struggled to raise her hand and I stopped.

Her words came out in a hoarse whisper. "It was...Jackson, wasn't...it?"

I bent over the bed, close to her face. "Yeah."

"How many...died?" It was such an effort for her to speak. I looked over my shoulder toward the door, wishing her mom or a nurse would come back into the room. Lindsey's gray eyes were wide open and determined.

"Too many," I breathed. "I think twenty-three kids and few teachers—Ms. Fletcher died, and so did Amber Lewis and Greg Sullivan." The names were thick on my tongue. To lose a favorite teacher and two of the most popular kids in school made it seem even more like a horrible nightmare.

Tears dribbled down Lindsey's cheeks. "He came for us. It's our fault," she whispered.

I sucked in a deep breath, shaking my head. "He was crazy. No one knows why he did it. He's dead, Lindsey. Aunt Reni shot him and he fell from the scaffolding in the theater storage room." I lowered my voice. "I don't think he told anyone."

Lindsey's head rocked back and forth. "You have to talk to Matthew—tell him what happened and explain to him why I can't meet up tonight." Her voice gained urgency and I stepped away from the bed. The blood drained from my face and I felt light headed.

The pitch of the monitor's beeping changed and two nurses rushed into the room. They blocked my view of Lindsey as they worked to calm her and check her vital signs.

I backed through the doorway and bumped into Mrs. Meade.

"Is she awake?" she asked. Her face lit up.

"Yes, just now..." I trailed off as Lindsey's mom pushed by me to reach her daughter.

The bright lights in the hallway made my head hurt and the back of my throat ached. Was Lindsey right—were we responsible for all those deaths?

Hands clasped my shoulders and I jumped. When I swung around, I wondered if it could get any worse.

"What are you doing here?" I hissed.

Hunter frowned and searched the corridor, before he

looked back at me. "I wanted to see how Lindsey was doing." He merely shrugged. "I couldn't believe it when my cousin said he'd heard she was in the hospital. There was so much blood, I thought she was a goner."

I grabbed Hunter's arm and pulled him to the elevator. Once the door shut behind us and we were alone, I faced him.

"You're not fooling anyone. You didn't even hang out with Lindsey. Why are you really here?"

His eyes flicked to the ceiling. When the elevator stopped and the door opened with a dinging noise, he muttered, "Maybe I came to see you."

His words shook my mind, but I didn't slow down as I stepped out of the elevator, crossed the lobby, and exited the hospital. I zipped up my coat and pulled mittens from the pockets. The wind whipped against my face, but the bitter chill was welcomed.

"I'm not stupid," I finally said. I stopped beside a van that afforded some protection from the wind, and turned on Hunter who was following on my heels. "We're not friends, either."

Hunter's hands were in his pockets and the gusts flapped his hood in the air. Snowflakes tumbled from the sky, speckling his hair with little white pebbles. He was a lot taller than me and when he moved closer, his body blocked even more of the wind. I was sixteen-years-old and a junior in high school, and I couldn't recall ever standing so close to a guy before, other than my dad or brother. But Hunter's demeanor wasn't romantic. It was more of a threatening gesture the way he loomed over me, his eyes sparking. I shrunk back into my coat.

"We barely escaped death together today. How can you say we aren't friends?"

I opened my mouth to speak and then smacked it shut. A couple huddled next to each other walked by. When they were out of earshot, I replied, "Maybe Jackson snapped because of us—because of what happened. It might be our fault that he killed all those kids." The air was so cold that the tears that pooled at the corners of my eyes disappeared into the wind.

Hunter closed the distance until he was only inches from my face. "That's not true. Jackson had a lot more problems than anything we did—or didn't do."

"Why are you really here?" I hated the squeak in my voice.

"Why is it so hard to believe I came to see you and Lindsey?" When my brows rose, he continued. "You two were always together, so I figured you'd be here."

His words swirled in the blustery air between us. My heart slowed and I chewed my lip. The cold was invading my coat, chilling me to the bone. Random visions of dead kids in the school's hallway weren't helping. I rubbed my temples in an attempt to erase the gory images from my mind.

I dared to meet Hunter's unwavering gaze. "You don't feel any guilt about what happened today?"

"Bad things happen to people all the time, and they don't pick up a gun and shoot up a bunch of people. Jackson was sick in the head. No, we can't blame ourselves—and you were just there because of Lindsey. You definitely shouldn't worry about anything. Besides, Jackson is dead. It's over."

The breath caught in my throat. "I do worry. My aunt is the sheriff. She never stops until she figures out every single angle. She's just like that. If she discovers I was there that night, she's going to kill me."

"So many of our friends died today, Taylor—Ms. Fletcher

and Mr. Dodgly too. It's a little shallow to be worrying about getting in trouble, don't you think?"

His words sunk in like the pounding of a sledgehammer. I gulped, unable to see Hunter through the tears. Without warning, he pulled me against his chest and hugged me. I almost squirmed out of his tight hold, but I was too tired to wrestle with him. He was right. How could I worry about Aunt Reni finding out about that night when our classmates and teachers were dead?

But I still couldn't stifle the fear that gripped my heart.

As I sagged against Hunter's chest, I couldn't forget Danielle's face when she had glared at me, or the smirk on the stranger's lips when he'd stepped out of the shadows.

Aunt Reni would eventually find out, and then I really was dead.

8

SERENITY

D aniel's lips lingered on mine and I didn't want to pull away. He smelled like wood smoke and leather this morning and the inside of his Jeep was warm. Just beyond the vehicle's windows were three inches of fresh snow from the night before with temperatures hovering in the teens. It wasn't even officially winter yet, and the weather had taken a turn from the chilly bright days of autumn. The icy conditions fit my mood for the day. Would it ever end—the barrage of senseless acts of violence?

As if he read my mind, Daniel caressed my shoulder and offered a small smile. "It will get better. It always does."

I puffed out my frustration and pulled my hat down lower on my head. "I wish I had your optimism. It's been one crime spree after another for over a year now. I think Blood Rock is cursed."

"Some of those crimes took place in other towns," Daniel pointed out.

"Then maybe it's just me. I'm the one who's cursed."

Daniel's face scrunched. "Don't say that. You're the one who solved all those crimes and stopped the bad guys from hurting more innocent people. I think you're the luckiest person around—the most blessed. Someone's watching over you, Serenity."

I rolled my eyes. This was one of the problems I had with Daniel. He really was a man of faith. I suspected it was his upbringing with the Amish, but whatever it was, I didn't share his rosy outlook about our fellow humans. I'd seen too much suffering and sick shit to think someone was watching over me or anyone else.

"I'd like to know where the Higher Authority you're talking about was when Miriam Coblenz and her groom were gunned down at their own wedding, along with her father and several other guests. Or when the serial killer, Caleb Johnson, killed and mutilated those poor Amish girls, and nearly killed CJ. And now this. Where was He when that psycho kid shot up his classmates and teachers? There's only chaos in the world," I argued.

Daniel sighed heavily and took my hand into his own. He touched the gem on the engagement ring he'd given me. "We've talked about this before. I've tried to explain, but I understand how you feel. Especially after everything you've seen and the actions you've had to take to keep this town safe."

I lowered my voice. "I'm just exhausted. Twenty-six people gone. This was the third most deadly school shooting in the United States. We just wrapped up the paperwork for Caleb Johnson's killing spree—and now this. Our little department can't keep up with so many calamities."

"Don't you have help from the outside on this one?"

"Of course, and I'm grateful for the feds' support, but they complicate matters."

"Well, at least this doesn't have anything to do with the Amish, for a change."

I snorted. "Yeah. There is that, at least."

I grabbed the door handle and Daniel stopped me. "Call me if you need anything. I'm in town today,"

I leaned over and kissed him lightly. His hand curled around the side of my face. "I love you, Serenity. Have faith that things will get better."

I exhaled. "You know, we'll have to delay the wedding."

He rubbed the black stubble on his chin. "Let's not make that call right now. If we have to catch a break to get married, we might never tie the knot."

I dropped my head back. "You just said things will get better, but now you admit it's never going to improve," I challenged.

He snorted softly. "Got me there." He continued in a nonchalant way. "I'm just saying we shouldn't put off the wedding. There isn't a mystery that you have to solve. There's no one in danger anymore." When I began to protest, he raised his finger and wagged it. "It's just a small ceremony in a couple of weeks, with a few close friends and family. We might as well get it over with."

This time I smiled. "That's so romantic, Daniel. I think I'm going to swoon."

"Hey, I'll be very romantic on our honeymoon when we're on that warm tropical beach."

The sideways grin he flashed at me spread warm honey through my belly. My heart fluttered. "Dammit, don't do that!"

"What am I doing?" His voice was velvet and one brow rose questioningly.

"You know exactly what I'm talking about." I flung the door open and stepped out into brisk air.

"Can we meet for lunch—or dinner—or I can bring you something to eat later?"

I huffed. He knew me so well. "I'll be tied up all day. I'll text you if I get a free moment."

I had closed the door and was about to walk away when the passenger window lowered and he called out, "I love you."

"I love you, too," I stuttered the words out and hurried to the sidewalk that led to the back entrance of the building. The usually vacant parking lot was packed with cars from out of state. I had spotted a crowd gathered at the front of the building and had asked Daniel to pull around back to avoid the questions and cameras.

I licked my lips thinking about how messed up I was as I slid in the back door and unzipped my jacket. I couldn't even tell my fiancé I loved him without stuttering. The idea of getting married made my heart gallop and tied my stomach in knots.

Rosie saw me and hurried over. She handed me a hot cup of coffee and I loved the red-headed receptionist for it. Before she could begin rambling on, I interrupted. "I've already been to the school this morning and I talked to the feds. The bodies should be released to the families this afternoon, except the shooter, we're holding him for a while longer. Grievance counsellors will be on hand at the middle school auditorium today. The press can get an update about the wounded at ten-thirty this morning at Blood Rock Regional Hospital, and Greater Union Memorial will update on the two victims that were taken there at noon. I'll have another press release for you by early afternoon, and I'll talk to reporters at five o'clock."

Rosie's head nodded as she crossed off items on her notepad.

"Very good, very good," she mumbled. "That takes care of about everything for the moment." I turned to leave and she spoke up. "Wait, here's a message from a lady in Indianapolis. Says she's looking for her sister who's gone missing. She thinks she might be in Blood Rock." She handed me the note.

It was such a mundane inquiry and yet, my muscles tightened as I stared down at the woman's name and number.

"Oh, and Toby Bryant is waiting in your office," she added.

Her words got me walking quickly down the hallway.

The school shooting didn't fall into the jurisdiction of the US Marshals Service, and the sudden appearance of my partner in a cold case that began in the Strasburg Amish community in Pennsylvania last summer, and ended with the Coblenz wedding massacre was not expected, to say the least.

When I came through the doorway, the tan cowboy hat was a welcome surprise. He greeted me with a lopsided smile and bright blue eyes. "Howdy, Sheriff," he said, tipping his hat.

I couldn't stop my smile from spreading. Toby was one of those charming country boy types, but underneath all that polite small-town persona was a damn good officer of the law. He certainly had no qualms about bending the rules on an investigation to get the job done, which made him even more likeable in my book.

I shook his hand and sat down across my desk from him. "What brings you to my neck of the woods, Toby?"

He removed the hat and set it on his lap. "Thought you might need some help around here." He offered a slight frown with raised brows. "You have a lot on your plate at the moment."

I nodded and tugged my ponytail tighter. "I've seen a hell of a lot, but this"—I let out a long breath—"is the worst I've ever experienced." I leaned over the desk. "All those poor innocent kids gunned down like animals. Unlike Brent Prowes, who opened fire at the Coblenz wedding reception because of a jealous infatuation with an Amish girl from his past, our shooter at the school doesn't appear to have any particular motive at all, except to kill as many of his classmates as possible."

Toby's gaze focused and I could clearly see his mind working. "There's always a motive, Sheriff, you and I both know that. It's just the figuring it out that keeps life interesting."

I glanced out the window. Snow flurries were dancing around in the wind. When I looked back at Toby, I dropped my voice without much thought. "We're following the usual leads—disgruntled relationship, bullying, problems at home—but haven't come up with anything solid at this time. The rifle was legally owned by his older brother, and stolen straight out of a gun cabinet that wasn't secured. The kid didn't use social media, so there's no trail there. And the students we've interviewed so far said that although Jackson Merritt didn't have many friends and wasn't popular, he wasn't threatening in any way. Everyone, from the teachers and office staff to the students, were shocked to hear he was the shooter."

"That's strange. Usually when there's mass shootings like this, people start coming out of the woodwork proclaiming they always suspected the shooter would act out sooner or later. Sometimes there's physical or sexual abuse, a broken home, or drug use involved. Then there are those cases where we're dealing with a true narcissistic personality. In most cases, there's that *yeah I saw it coming with that guy* moment."

I tapped my fingers onto the desk and Toby sat back in the seat, waiting.

"There is something that's got me perplexed and maybe

even a little spooked." Toby tilted his head. He still looked relaxed, but there was a subtle change in his stance. Curiosity had made him alert. "The shooter's MO changed after he reloaded a second magazine. His desire to kill as many people as possible was interrupted." Toby's brows rose higher. "He focused on one or possibly two teens, going to great lengths to follow them into a quieter part of the school." I took a chance, trusting the Marshal. "One of the kids was my niece, and I don't think she's being entirely honest with me about her connection to the shooter."

"I see." He rubbed his chin, his gaze on a faraway imaginary place.

I let him have his moment to think about what I'd just said, trying to be as cool as he was.

His eyes locked on mine. "It's never enough for me to find and arrest a fugitive. I want to know what made that particular person commit the crimes they did. The journey to discover their secrets is what my job is all about."

"That's how I feel," I said. "There's more to this tragedy than just a troubled teen with a gun."

"But you're afraid if you dig too deep, you might uncover something that will damage your niece."

I nodded reluctantly. "If I don't at least try to find the answers to those questions, someone else might get hurt."

"You think your shooter has a connection to another crime?"

"Call it a gut instinct, because I don't have anything else to go on." I took a sip of my coffee, savoring the strong, warm liquid in my mouth.

"I know you, Sheriff. You won't be able to sleep at night if you don't follow your gut." He shrugged. "Who knows, there might not be anything nefarious going on with your niece after all, but it's a gamble you need to take to discover the truth."

I met his somber gaze and inclined my head. "Why are you really here, Marshal? I find it hard to believe John is wasting manpower on an event that the FBI and the locals have jurisdiction over."

He grunted. "I'm on vacation."

"Are you serious—you're spending your precious time off here in Blood Rock because of a school massacre?"

Toby put his hat back on and pressed it down just right. "I don't have a girlfriend, wife, or kids, very little family, and a handful of busy friends. It seemed like the right thing to do, coming here to assist you in any way you might need." He winked. "Besides, I recall a certain Sheriff coming to Pennsylvania with me and my partner to solve a cold case while she was on her vacation."

I smirked. "Got me there."

"So, what can I do for you, Sheriff? I'm at your service."

My cheeks warmed and I really hoped Toby didn't see me blushing. He was an attractive man, with a wiry, athletic frame and boyish grin. His mustache and the light shading of two-day old stubble on his chin made him look like he'd just stepped out of an old western movie. But it was the Texan accent that often made tingles creep over my skin when he spoke. I blinked, taking a quick breath. "Actually, I'm glad you showed up." I handed him the memo Rosie had given me in the hallway. "I'm completely booked up with the school shooting, so I won't have time to look into this, and you're pretty good at tracking people down, right?"

"Yes, Ma'am. That's what I do best." He tipped his hat. "I'll get right on this."

"Talk to Rosie. There's a vacant desk and an extra computer in the corner of the front room. Make yourself comfortable, and let me know if you need anything."

"I sure will." He said it in a polite way, but there was something more to the smoothness of his tone. I almost thought he was flirting.

Toby passed Todd coming in as he left the room. "Do you have a moment, boss?"

I glanced at my watch. "Just one. I have to meet with Bobby and then get back to the school."

"I got the list of convicted and suspected drug dealers in the area you requested." He handed it to me and I began to slide the paper into a folder on my desk. "You might want to take a look at it before you leave." His voice was edgy and his square jaw set. "Danielle Brown died of what appeared to be an accidental overdose on heroin and fentanyl. Everyone on that list was either dealing cocaine or heroin, or both."

My time with Toby had seriously put me behind schedule and I was anxious to get moving, but Todd's worried look made me hesitate and lift the paper. I scanned it twice and paused.

"You've got to be kidding me."

"I wish I were." He shifted his weight from one foot to the other. "Does that mean you'll be adding the Amish community to your agenda for today?"

Visions of buggies and beards sprinkled my mind. I shook my head. "It will have to be tomorrow, but yes, it seems a trip out to the settlement is warranted."

I folded the paper and stuffed it in my pocket. I inwardly groaned when I thought about the bishop and what he was going to say when I showed up.

9

TAYLOR

My little car bounced up the pitted driveway, splashing through icy puddles. I slowed to avoid hitting a chicken and parked in front of the white farmhouse. Tentacles of smoke rose from the chimney into the cold air. I breathed in the burning wood smell.

Two girls were picking up logs on the front porch. They were dressed the same in greenish-blue dresses that reminded me of the ocean. The bottoms of their dresses flapped in the wind, along with the strings on their white caps. I hadn't been to the Amish community in a while. Seeing the girls in their odd clothes reminded me of my only Amish friend. Her name was Naomi and she'd fallen in love with my brother, Will. They were going to run away to Montana together to join the rodeo and live happily ever after. But she was murdered and never got the chance to go. She was shot dead in a cornfield by a crazy, jealous teenager, like Jackson. Only that boy had been Amish. As far as I knew, he was locked up in some prison far away.

I shivered. Aunt Reni sometimes said she thought Blood Rock was cursed. Maybe it was. As I climbed the stairs, I thought about Naomi's mischievous smile and contagious laughter. It had taken her a little while to open up, but once she had, she seemed like any other teenage girl. Yet, she *was* different. She was secretive and suspicious, always worried that someone was spying on her.

One of the girls jumped when she turned around and I saw me. She must not have heard my car through the howling wind. Her doe eyes rounded and a snowflake caught on her lash, but she couldn't wipe it away because her hands were full of logs.

"Do you need help?" I offered.

"No, no, I'm good," she said quickly. Her rosy cheeks were plump and I guessed she was around nine years old. The smaller girl just stared at me with her mouth gaping. She was a replica of her older sister.

"Is your brother home?" I tried to sound conversational, but my heart trembled and I felt sick.

"Which one?" she asked.

I had to smile at my stupidity. The Amish almost always had huge families. This girl might have five or six brothers for all I knew. "Matthew. Matthew Troyer," I repeated.

She nodded vigorously and jutted her chin toward the barn I had passed. "He's feeding the horses. You'll find him there."

"Thank you," I mumbled. I trotted down the steps, leaving the girls and their curious stares behind.

I stretched my legs and pulled my scarf tighter, then slipped on my mittens. The temperature was dropping and snow was beginning to accumulate. If I didn't hurry, I might not make it home. The thought of what Mom would do if I slid off the road into the ditch, and she had to drive all the way out here to get me made me move even faster.

The sliding door was cracked open and I pushed on it until there was enough room for me to slip through. I blinked at the dimness inside and sneezed into the puff of dust that enveloped me.

"What are you doing here?"

The voice was a harsh whisper. Matthew pushed by me and shut the door completely. My heart hammered harder when I realized we were alone. A horse whinnied, drawing my attention, and I gratefully walked away from Matthew's angry face to pet the black head hanging over the stall door.

"I'm sorry. I didn't think it would be a big deal, and I had something to tell you." I risked a glance over my shoulder. Matthew's face had loosened. He looked back at me with a neutral expression. "Did you hear about the school shooting?"

He nodded, sticking his hands in the pockets of his black corduroy coat. "How's Lindsey taking it?"

I realized with a jolt he had no idea she had been shot. He was Amish after all. He didn't carry a cell phone or drive a car with a radio in it. No television, either. Everyone in town knew what had happened minutes after the first shots were fired, but not the Amish. They had to wait for information to trickle in from drivers and other outsiders' mouths.

My eyes widened and it was like seeing Matthew for the first time. His pants were a deepest blue that looked homespun and I would bet his mother had made the knitted black hat on his head. Brown hair flared out from under the cap and freckles sprinkled his nose. His eyes were the same muddy brown color as his sisters. I decided that he was kind of attractive and I understood what Lindsey saw in him.

"She was shot, Matt." His mouth opened and his faced paled. "She's okay," I rushed out, "She's in the hospital and she asked me to come tell you what had happened." I looked away. It was easier to stare at the pretty horse that was stretching its neck out to me for more petting, than to deal with Matthew's stricken expression. "She didn't want you to think she had stood you up last night or was ignoring your calls."

He moved closer. "How bad are her injuries?"

"I don't know all the details, but a bullet grazed her head." His eyes grew to saucer size. "But the doctor says she should recover fully. She'll be in the hospital for a while, doing therapy and stuff."

Matthew crossed the aisle and sunk down onto a bale of hay.

Losing all nerve to talk anymore to him, I said, "I did what Lindsey asked me to do. I'll leave you alone."

I was almost to the door and could feel the icy wind blowing through the slight gap when he called out, "No, wait. Don't go yet."

I slowly turned back and walked toward him. "What?"

He raised his face. "Is it true that it was Jackson who killed all those people?"

Matthew was a year older than me, but at that moment, there was an innocence about him that made me feel much older. I watched snippets of the news and watched horror and crime movies. Violence wasn't completely foreign to me, even though what had happened at the school was hard for me to wrap my head around. I could see in Matthew's eyes that he didn't even begin to comprehend what had happened or more importantly, why.

I took a deep breath. There was enough space on the hay bale that I joined Matthew. "Yeah, it was Jackson. Twenty-six people lost their lives yesterday—mostly kids. Some were friends of mine. Lindsey's lucky to be alive, and so am I." I faced Matthew. "I was with Hunter, and I think Jackson was coming after us. If it weren't for my Aunt Reni, we'd probably be dead, too. She shot Jackson and he died falling from the high place where we were hiding. He almost reached us."

"Sheriff Serenity saved the day again, huh? I met her, you know. When the Amish girls were killed by the English driver. My brother, Abner, courted one of the girls—Makayla."

"Why would she talk to you about it?"

"She interviewed everyone in the community. Bishop Esch set it all up." He raised a single brow. "She noticed me somehow. It was like she saw into my soul and knew that I was being reckless."

I shuddered once. "Aunt Reni is good at her job. She senses things about people and it helps her solve crimes." I pressed my lips together and forced myself to meet Matthew's curious stare. "The problem is she might be onto us"—I motioned with my hands—"all of us. She might find out about that night."

"That's why Jackson shot up the school?" he whispered.

I nodded slowly. "Maybe."

Matthew thudded his head back against the wall. I took his lack of words as an opportunity to make my escape. I'd told him about Lindsey and he also knew about Jackson. He was a smart kid, and he was Amish. He could keep a secret.

He jumped up, following me. "Wait!"

I slowed, but didn't stop. I wanted to go home—to get away from the dark, drafty barn and the Amish boy who reminded me of sweet Naomi.

"I want to visit Lindsey," he said. "Will you drive me?"

I paused without turning. "Your parents would allow that?"

"I'll arrange something. They won't know where I'm going."

Heat spread from my stomach upward, until my face was flaming hot. I rounded on him. "No more lies and sneaking around! I'm finished with it all." He opened his mouth to interrupt me and I pointed my finger, raising my voice to cut him off. "No, Matthew. A girl died because of us."

"It was her fault! She made her own choices," he shouted back.

I cringed. What if his mother or father appeared in the doorway? I needed to get out of there, but I paused long enough to look fiercely at him. "If you had any sense at all, you'd stay away from Lindsey and she'd stay away from you." Hurt lit his eyes, but I ignored his pain and barreled on. "It will never work between you two. It's doomed to end in a horrible way. Trust me, I know. Amish and English aren't supposed to fall in love. Get out now, before it's too late."

I barely felt the biting wind on my face as I stomped through the snow to my car. But I did feel the hot tears running down my cheeks.

10

SERENITY

"What do you have for me, Bobby?" I raised the mask over my mouth. The smell of formaldehyde churned my stomach and I hoped to avoid the nausea if at all possible.

Bobby pulled his mask down and removed his gloves. I waited while he washed his hands and picked up his old-school notebook.

"You're going to have to start using the tablet," I scolded. "Or you're going to get in trouble with the state."

He made a growling noise and ignored my comment all together. He pulled back the white sheet and stood over Jackson Merritt. I approached the body with slow steps. This young man had killed more than two dozen people and critically wounded several more. Mostly, I loathed the sight of him, but the pimples on his forehead and chin were distracting. They reminded me that he was only kid, and that made hating him harder.

"The rushed toxicology report already came back. He

wasn't under the influence of any kind of drug or alcohol. His system was clean," Bobby said.

"I'm not surprised. His methodical approach to entering the school, snapping the weapon together and reloading, proved he had a fairly sound body. His mind is another story altogether."

"After everything we've experienced, do you still not believe that evil is all around us, Serenity?"

I rolled my eyes. My coroner was beginning to sound like Bishop Aaron Esch. If I didn't know better, I'd think he'd once been Amish.

"Let's not get into that discussion again," I scoffed. "Yes, I believe in evil, but I think men and women are inherently evil. There's a lot of crazy souls out there that are just waiting to lose control and commit terrible acts. There's no magical being making people kill each other."

Bobby looked at me over the top of his glasses, and my mind drifted back to a conversation I had with the bishop a couple of months earlier when we'd discovered Makayla Bowman's body in the shed.

A chill raced up my spine. The faint smell of blood still hung in the air. Not so long ago, right where we stood, Makayla had been tortured and murdered.

"What are you saying?"

The bishop snapped, "Satan was in this room. He did this—and he's out there, Sheriff."

The solid sound of Bobby's voice brought me back to the bright lights of the examination room. "I have twenty-six bodies in several morgues, most of which are teenagers." He twirled the end of his white mustache. "There's no way to explain that kind of savagery. Especially when it's committed by another teen."

I sighed and looked closer at Jackson Merritt. He was ordinary in every way, except his name would go down in infamy on the list of the deadliest school shooters in America. I shook my head and returned my gaze to Bobby.

"There's nothing wrong with trying to figure out why this kid did what he did." I rolled my neck, popping it. It wasn't even noon yet and I was already exhausted. "We might never know for sure what made this kid snap. You were all for the psychoanalysis of the serial killer on our last investigation."

Bobby's brow furrowed. "That was different. Our killer had very specific victims and motives. We were able to compare him to other serial killers. The molds for mass shooters are different—they come from all walks of life. The randomness of it is what disturbs me most. There is no way Jackson Merritt had a grudge against all the people he killed. He was going for shock value."

"Perhaps..." I trailed off and removed the mask. "Sorry to run, but I'm meeting officials at the school."

"There is something else, but it might take a few days to get conclusive results." Bobby motioned me over to the counter, where a flannel shirt coat was folded and enclosed in a plastic evidence bag. "The shooter was wearing this at the time of his rampage." He pointed at the pocket with his pencil. "There was some white powdery residue inside—only a miniscule amount, but the texture of it reminded me of heroin."

I raised my brows and he hurried on, "Not personal experience, I dare say. We've had enough drugs come through here that I consider my knowledge quite reliable."

I frowned. "I was only kidding, Bobby. If that's true, it only complicates the investigation, giving me another reason to visit the Amish community as soon as possible."

Bobby folded his glasses and set them down. "What on earth do the Amish have to do with this mess?"

"Three words—drugs and Monroe Swarey."

11

TAYLOR

Snow began falling harder as I pulled out onto the roadway. I leaned forward over the steering wheel and turned the windshield wipers on high speed. I couldn't see the lines on the road anymore, and my tire tracks were the first ones cutting through the thin blanket of snow forming on the road. I shouldn't have driven out here when the weather was worsening. I was a mess from the meeting with Matthew Troyer, and tears bubbled up in my eyes when my mind drifted back to the carnage in the school's hallway. Had it been only yesterday that Jackson entered the school and began shooting everyone?

My hands started to shake on the steering wheel and I squinted, trying to see through the giant flakes hitting the windshield. I saw the stop sign at the last second and hit the brakes. They locked up and my car slid sideways. I frantically pumped the brakes, but they wouldn't catch. Even though the car was moving fairly slowly, I still gasped as I tried helplessly to stop. There was a thump and the car dipped and rolled into the snow-covered bank. My seat belt pressed uncomfortably into my chest, but at least the airbags didn't deploy.

I blew out a wobbly breath and grabbed my cellphone from my tote bag. The battery was dead.

"I'm so stupid," I muttered. I zipped up my coat, put my mittens back on and pushed the door open. Snowflakes melted on my face as I shut the door and walked to the front of the car. A tire was stuck in the ditch and without the help of a tow truck, the car wasn't going anywhere anytime soon. There was a small dent where the front end pressed into the bank, but that was the only real damage to the car.

"Mom and Dad are going to kill me." The words puffed out into the cold air.

It was nearly dark, and a herd of cows with snow blanketing their backs stood beside the road, watching me. The only other sign of life was a flickering light in the distance. I guessed it to be closer than trying to walk back to the Troyer farm. After the things I'd said and the fact that I shouldn't have even gone there in the first place, I figured I wouldn't be welcome to return there anyway. I stood for a minute, shivering in the falling snow. The icy chill on my cheeks was like a hundred pin pricks, but the pain felt good in a way. At least I was alive to feel it. I clenched my fists and pressed my cracked lips together. I tried not to pity myself, but it had been a rough couple of days.

A cow mooed and it seemed as if she was telling me to get moving. With a heavy heart and very little energy, I began trudging along the road, toward the light on the hill.

The walk seemed to take forever, but it probably only lasted ten minutes when I finally reached the front porch of the small white house beside the road. There was another larger house further back up the long driveway, but I was already frozen and I didn't think my legs would take me farther.

There wasn't a door bell so I knocked several times and waited. The scent of chimney smoke wafted on the wind, creating an almost magical feeling to the snowy countryside. When the door cracked open, I straightened.

A short Amish woman peeked out. Some of her gray hair had escaped from under her cap and the hunter green dress she wore was splattered with flour.

"Do you need help?" the woman asked.

I tried to hide my smile. I'm sure she wasn't expecting an English girl to be on her porch. "Yes, I had a little accident back there—slid right into a ditch—and my phone is dead." Her eyes widened and I added, "I mean the battery—it's dead. Can I use your telephone to call a tow truck?"

"Oh, my, what bad luck you've had this night." She flung the door wide open and shuffled me into the house. "Of course you may use the telephone, but it's not in the house." She shut the door and called out something in her language before turning her attention back to me. She opened a door to a closet and pulled out a white towel. She handed it to me and led me down the hallway. "We share a telephone with my daughter, and it's in a shed halfway up the hillside. You should dry off and warm yourself with a cup of hot cocoa before you go to make your call."

I rubbed the towel onto my wet hair and let out a breath when the stuffy warmth inside the small house began to penetrate my skin. When we stepped into the kitchen, I wrinkled my nose at the unfamiliar odor of the gas lamps hanging from the ceiling. They were strange looking contraptions, with live, dancing flames in each one. The room was relatively small, and the counter was piled high with Tupperware containers and tin pie trays. The odd smell of the lamps was quickly replaced by that of baking cinnamon and sugar. I inhaled deeply.

"It smells like a bakery in here," I exclaimed.

The woman smiled back. "The community is having a benefit dinner and sale tomorrow for our minister, James Hooley, who's been battling cancer. It's a dreadful disease and his family needs help with the medical bills." She spread her arms wide. "It's my job to make the apple pies for the event—with assistance from my Sarah."

I followed the nod of her head. A girl about my age came out of another room, carrying a crate filled to the brim with apples. She dropped the crate onto the table and wiped her hands on the sides of her maroon dress. "Hello," Sarah said.

"Hi," I replied. "How many pies do you have to make?"

"We're aiming for twenty-two, right Mam?" Sarah took an apple out of the bin and took a bite out of it. She tossed me one, and I scrambled with cold hands to grab it from the air. "Good catch!" Sarah said.

For the first time in two days, I felt like smiling. The tall girl had dark brown hair and sparkling green eyes. Her lips curled up in a carefree grin that put me completely at ease in the strangers' house.

"Sarah, dear, can you give this poor girl"—she looked confused and turned to me—"what is your name, child?"

"Taylor," I said.

"How rude of me not to make introductions. It's not often we have unexpected visitors we don't know." She dipped her head. "I'm Anna Bachman, and this is my granddaughter."

"Nice to meet you both," I chirped. My mind raced and I asked, "Are you related to Daniel Bachman?"

Mrs. Bachman laughed softly, but her eyes focused on me with hawkish interest. "I'm his mother, and Sarah here, is his niece."

"What a small world." I rushed the words out excitedly. "He's marrying my Aunt Reni."

"Sheriff Adams is your aunt?" Mrs. Bachman exchanged a surprised glance with Sarah.

"Yep, the one and only."

"So, you're Taylor Johnson." Sarah said the words as a statement instead of a question. By the expression of her knitted brow, she was remembering something. The intense look made my stomach tighten a little.

"Then you will be like family to us in a couple short weeks, Taylor," Mrs. Bachman tilted her head and stared at me.

"I guess that's true. But with everything going on with the school shooting and all, I wouldn't be surprised if the wedding was postponed—at least that's what my mom thinks."

"Oh, yes. That was a terrible thing to happen, but I hope Daniel and Serenity don't put it off too long." She leaned over and nudged me with her elbow. "Those two aren't getting any younger and if they're going to have children, they best start right away."

My eyes bulged and my mouth dropped open.

Sarah laughed. "Mam, you mustn't talk of such things. I believe you've startled Taylor."

"Well, it's the truth. They act more like silly teenagers than adults when it comes to courting," Mrs. Bachman shot back. "If your uncle doesn't corral that woman soon, she's likely to get away."

"Whoa...children?" I found my voice. "You think Aunt Reni is going to have kids someday?"

Mrs. Bachman and Sarah frowned at me.

"Of course. Why wouldn't she?" Mrs. Bachman said in a firm voice.

I squirmed in my coat. For a second there I'd forgotten that Mrs. Bachman was Amish. Her grandmotherly expectations were probably higher than other people's. I tried really hard to keep my face expressionless, but I was close to throwing my head back and laughing. Mrs. Bachman was Daniel's mom, though. I didn't want to offend her.

"You know that my aunt is the sheriff in town. She's very busy, like all the time, with important stuff." Mrs. Bachman's eyes narrowed and the sweet-looking old lady abruptly reminded me of a bird of prey. I cleared my throat. "Well, yeah. I'm sure she'll have a baby eventually..." I trailed off, taking a long breath.

"I wonder if they've even discussed having children?" Mrs. Bachman shook her head. "My boy wants a family, this I know. What a disappointment it would be to lose the opportunity if the sheriff isn't interested."

Mrs. Bachman glanced back at me and I flinched, keeping my mouth shut.

When I didn't say anything, the old woman shrugged. "I have my own worries. These pies aren't going to make themselves." With a sudden change of mood, Mrs. Bachman turned to Sarah with a cheerful voice. "Dear, let's warm Taylor up with some hot cocoa, while I run to the storeroom to get the lard."

"That's really nice of you, but I have to call a tow truck company and pull my car out of the ditch. I have to get home."

"I'm sure the sheriff or even Daniel will come to your aid. You shouldn't be driving in this frightful weather," Mrs. Bachman admonished.

"Oh, no. No, I wouldn't want to bother either of them. I can take care of this myself." The last thing I needed was for Aunt Reni to find out I drove to the Amish community. She'd have a million questions, all of which I didn't want to answer.

Mrs. Bachman's face hardened, but didn't argue with me, thank goodness. "All right then, Sarah, please take her to the shed so she can make her call." She stepped up and gave me a quick hug. "I'll pray for your safe travel home."

"I'll see you at the wedding."

She pulled back. Her face was shadowed. "We won't be there, child. My son chose a different path from us, and some things can't be undone. It is our way, but I'm sure we'll see you again."

When Sarah and I stepped out into the night, I inhaled the cold air.

"Sorry about my Mam," Sarah said. She pressed in closer as we made our way up the icy driveway. "She's opinionated."

I glanced over at her and she was grinning broadly. Laughter bubbled up into my mouth. "You look a little like him."

"Who?" She asked.

"Daniel. You two have the same hair and your eyes are shaped alike. I should have seen the resemblance when I first saw you."

"Everyone says my mom looks a lot like Uncle Daniel." She paused, breathing harder. "What's he like?"

"You don't know him?"

She shrugged. "Not very well. I only met him for the first time last year. I was a baby when he left our people. We didn't see him all those years."

I scrunched my face into the sharp wind. "Wow. That's

crazy. I'd heard something about him being shunned, but I guess I didn't really understand exactly what it meant."

We reached the white-sided building, and Sarah flung the door aside. She busied herself with the lamp until it was lit and then closed the door. The small room had a table with a few chairs around it. The phone was on the wall.

"It was worse for Uncle Daniel." Sarah's breath streamed out in front of her, and I thought how most people's phone conversations were probably pretty short in here during the winter months. "He had joined the church and was even courting a girl when he decided to leave."

I leaned against the wall. My fingers were already numbing, and I wondered if Mom and Dad were worried about me, but my curiosity got the better of me. "So, if you aren't a member of the church, you can leave without being shunned."

"It's not as simple as that, but it definitely makes it easier."

I took a chance on trusting Sarah. "Has Matthew Troyer joined the church?"

Sarah's brow shot up, but her voice wasn't offended when she answered. "Not yet. He's supposed to join at the same time I do, this coming spring sometime."

"I see..."

"You know, it'll never work out between your friend and him."

I could feel the blood drain from my face. "How do you know about that?"

The corner of her mouth lifted. "I grew up with Matthew. All the kids talk. It's not a secret to us—only the adults."

I let out a breath, and with it released a lot of tension. I had more in common with this Amish girl I'd just met than with a lot of my other friends. And we agreed about Lindsey and Matthew and their doomed relationship.

"You're right. It's a huge mistake for Lindsey to mess around with Matthew. Look what happened to Naomi Beiler." I met her gaze, feeling the sting of tears welling up in the corners of my eyes.

Sarah came closer and her lips trembled. "Don't think about such a sad thing. Naomi was my friend, even though she was a few years older than me. She was always kind and she was very funny." She smiled fondly. "She could actually tell jokes and make me laugh." Her expression darkened. "She had a wild streak, and she wasn't happy with our people. We all figured she'd go English, but none of us kids thought she'd die in the process." She shook her head and frowned deeply. "David Lapp was not right in the head. He never was, even when he was little. I remember him catching a bird during recess one day. The poor thing had flown into a school window and laid stunned on the ground when he picked it up. Before anyone could stop him, he'd twisted its neck, killing it. He said he'd done it to end the bird's suffering—I knew better. He enjoyed killing that bird, same as he did killing Naomi."

I forgot about the cold as her words settled in my mind. I thought about Jackson, and wondered if he'd ever hurt animals or birds before he went on his shooting spree. Jackson Merritt and David Lapp were both messed up teenagers who killed people. One was Amish and the other was not.

When I looked back at Sarah, I found her waiting. There was a look of expectancy on her face.

"I don't want anything bad to happen to Lindsey. She survived the shooting at the school, yet I'm afraid that her secret relationship with Matthew could get her into trouble."

Sarah moved to peek out the doorway and then returned. Her movements were quick and agitated, making me nervous.

She took my hands and pulled me closer. "It's not safe for your friend to come around here. Promise me you'll keep her away."

She pivoted and went through the door.

"Wait!" I ran after her. "What do you mean?"

She turned around and held her finger to her mouth. "Hush, Taylor. I won't speak of this now, but don't say I didn't warn you."

I was left alone in the falling snow, with the heaviness of worry pressing into me. I had the same feeling that autumn night that seemed like a million years ago. When I closed my eyes, the snow had disappeared and was replaced by softly falling leaves and the smell of campfire smoke.

"She said she wanted the good stuff," Matthew argued with Hunter.

"I thought it was just some pot she wanted." He ran his hands through his hair in a tugging motion. "We should go with her."

"What's the big deal? Her brother went with her," Mathew replied. His hand snaked around Lindsey's waist and I glanced away.

"Jackson's not her brother," Hunter said.

"Lindsey, we should get going," I begged.

"Aww, come on, don't be such a party pooper," she told me.

"I've had enough, Lindsey. I'm leaving and you better come with me," I said.

"Yeah, let's go," Hunter chimed in.

"No one's going anywhere," a voice called out from the shadows.

I held my breath as the newcomer walked into the clearing.

12

SERENITY

When I walked through the door into my office, I was greeted by the sight of the US Marshal leaning back in my chair. The cowboy hat covered his face and his feet were crossed up on my desk.

"What do you think you're doing?" I demanded.

Toby woke up and pushed his hat back. He swung his feet down and rolled the chair closer to the desk. "You're welcome."

I wasn't in the mood for his games. Early morning wasn't the best time to try my patience, especially with the crap I was currently dealing with. I took the seat across from him and grunted. "What am I thanking you for?"

"Delivering another mystery to your doorstep," he said.

"Stop fooling around and spit it out."

He rolled his eyes. "I really hope you don't reserve that kind of harsh tone for your friends, otherwise you won't be making any new ones," he said, smirking. The look I leveled on him made him slump back a bit and the playfulness was gone from his face. "All right. Here it is." He handed me a piece of paper.

"Your missing lady is Charlene Noble. I talked to her sister yesterday and did a little more research on her." When he paused briefly, I flicked my wrist for him to continue. "The family used to live in Blood Rock, but they moved to Indianapolis about ten years ago. Charlene maintained contact with a close friend here, though. A few months ago, she returned to Blood Rock to help that same friend in need—at least, that's why her sister suspected she came back."

"Who is the mystery person she returned for?" Toby's theatrics made the blood pound through my veins. This wasn't the time to be giddy about a case—unless he thought it was something that I'd find very interesting.

"Her maiden name is Erin Knight. I think you might know her better by her married name." He paused for effect. "Swarey. Erin Swarey." He leaned back, lacing his hands behind his head. "Does that name ring any bells?"

More like explosions going off in my mind, I thought. "Hell, yeah. She's missing too," I said.

"From the cat-caught-the-mouse look on your face, I guess you've already read the Swarey files?" I took a swig of my coffee.

"Sure did." Toby watched me closely as he spoke. "Fascinating lifestyle for an Amish family, don't you think? The boy's a drug dealer, the father has anger management issues, and the formerly English mom has been missing for a few months. Sounds like a good mystery to me."

"You aren't kidding." I stared out the window. The snow had stopped during the night, and it looked like a winter wonderland in Blood Rock. Looks were deceiving, though. It was more like a town touched by evil and mayhem. I gazed back at Toby. "I was planning to head out to the country this afternoon to talk to Monroe anyway." Toby's brows rose and I explained. "Todd compiled a list of all our known drug dealers in the county. Jackson Merritt, our shooter, had a foster sister who died from an overdose of heroin, laced with fentanyl. At the time, we weren't able to trace the drugs to a seller"—I rubbed the back of my stiff neck—"and to be honest, we've been inundated with overdoses this past year. It's difficult to keep up. But with the connection to our school shooter, we wanted to take a deeper look into it."

"And you think Monroe Swarey might be our guy?"

"It's hard say. Over the past summer, he was fooling around with marijuana, nothing as hard as cocaine or heroin. He was a minor at the time, but if my memory serves me correctly, he's eighteen by now."

"October sixteenth, actually," Toby said, without even looking at his notes.

I nodded. "He's squirrelly, and I got the feeling that he'd be going after bigger game eventually." I crossed my arms on the desk. "I was a little preoccupied tracking down a serial killer, who was leaving a trail of mutilated Amish girls in his wake. Once I eliminated Monroe from the suspect list, I didn't give him much more thought. Until now."

"He was a suspect in those killings?" Toby's voice curled with energy.

"He was on my list, along with his father, Nicolas Swarey. The main reason being that his wife had up and disappeared, which is strange in their culture—and the dead dogs didn't help him any."

"Yes, I saw that in your notes. He shot them for attacking his livestock, and then dismembered them. The part about sawing up the bed and burning it in the yard probably triggered your suspicion as well."

"Yeah, that too," I mused.

"The father's behavior was psychopathic. It's understandable why he was on your radar."

"When we got our man, charges were dropped against Nicolas Swarey. The judge ordered him to take anger management counseling. From the paperwork I got back, he participated and passed with flying colors."

"Another sign of a psychopath—the uncanny ability to manipulate others."

I exhaled. I had only gotten a few hours of sleep the night before. The school shooting was unlike any other criminal investigation I'd handled in Blood Rock. Between juggling forensics for twenty-seven people, the media, the mayor, and clumsily attempting to sooth the spirits of the entire community, I was worn out.

"I just assumed the poor woman ran off to get away from her crazy husband and his lifestyle. She had grown up like you and me, and because of a schoolgirl crush, had ended up living like an Amish woman for over sixteen years. Who could blame her if she skipped out on her husband and son, maybe even escaped with another man?" I tapped my fingers. "If she had done that, you'd think she would have contacted an old friend to help her out in the crisis. Now this tantalizing information surfaces that the friend she probably contacted has disappeared too? That can't be a coincidence."

"That's exactly what I was thinking."

I glanced at the wall clock. "I'm tight on time today, but I think I can squeeze in a visit with the Swareys after the news conference this afternoon."

"I'll be ready." Toby stood up.

"Are you sure you wouldn't rather be on a beach somewhere, drinking a margarita?"

He snickered. "And miss out on the opportunity to mingle with the Amish again. Not a chance."

"Thanks, Toby. I really appreciate it. We're shorthanded and having you on board might make a big difference in finding out what happened to Erin Swarey and Charlene Noble."

When the door closed, I crossed the office to the window and looked out. "What about Taylor—how does my niece figure into this mess?" I muttered.

13

TAYLOR

"But the roads are clear now, Mom," I argued. Mom's hands were on her hips and she blocked the doorway. "Where did that dent in the front of your car come from?"

"I slid in the parking lot and bumped into the shopping cart rake," I lied. "It's not even that big. The engine is perfectly fine."

"That's not the point, Taylor. You've been gone a lot lately, and after what happened at the school, I think you should be spending more time at home with family."

The corner of Mom's mouth twitched. She looked like she might cry. I felt bad, but I had arranged a meeting and I couldn't miss it. I crossed the room and hugged her. "Don't worry. I'll be home before dark. I want to lay some flowers at the memorial, and there's a group counseling session I'm going to." I stepped back. "I think it will good for me to talk about things with the other kids."

She hesitated and I held my breath. When she moved

aside, I grabbed my tote and slipped by her before she could change her mind. "Thanks, Mom."

"Be careful! There might still be some slick spots on the road," she called out as I was closing the door.

The sun peeked out from behind the clouds, making the crusty snow sparkle. The rays of light erased a little bit of the nightmare of the past few days. As I climbed into my car, I admitted nothing had changed. It was about to get worse.

Hunter waved from across the diner and I hurried over to him. Nancy's Diner was packed. I noticed a lot of unfamiliar faces, along with the usual customers.

"Hey, girl. Are you meeting your aunt?"

I stopped and turned to Nancy. Her dyed red hair was coiled neatly on top of her head. The amount of makeup she wore was distracting. "No, not today. I'm with a friend."

Her gaze followed mine and her eyes widened. "Oh, I see." She leaned in closer. "Got yourself a nice-looking young man, Taylor."

"He's just a friend." I shook my head.

The side of her mouth lifted up and she dipped her head. "All right. If that's what you say." She nodded to another table. "There's some reporters over there that are about driving me crazy. I was hoping she'd take care of them for me."

I began to ease away from the restaurant owner. "If I see her, I'll tell her to stop by." I spun away, trying to avoid a drawn-out conversation with the older woman.

I ducked into the booth and finally let out a breath.

"What's wrong?" Hunter asked.

I glanced up. His brows were furrowed and his face was pale. I was willing to bet that he hadn't gotten a lot of sleep lately.

"It's been a long morning." When the petite, brown-haired waitress stopped at the table, I quickly ordered a cola and small fries.

"Is that all you're going to eat? I'll pay," Hunter offered.

"I'm not really hungry." I blinked. "Why are you being so nice to me?"

"Is it a crime to be polite?"

"Of course not, but you hardly ever spoke to me before."

"Before the shooting that left a bunch of our friends dead or injured? Before we ran for our lives together through the school?" He pressed his lips together and crossed his arms on the table. "We're not exactly strangers anymore."

"I was thinking more like before Danielle Brown ODed."

Silence was thick in the booth. Hunter stared at me with a furrowed brow for several long seconds. When he finally spoke, his voice was rough. "What do you want from me?

I slumped forward. "I think we should tell Aunt Reni about what happened that night."

"Are you crazy?" He looked around and lowered his voice. "It's over and done with. Danielle made her own stupid choice at the cost of her life. That's not our problem."

My face was on fire. "We were there and so was Jackson. Maybe that's why he did what he did?"

"Does it really matter? He's dead, Danielle's dead, and a whole lot of other people are dead. It won't bring anyone back."

"Those drugs killed Danielle. We can stop something like that from happening again."

Hunter ran his hand through his hair with a tug. "I'm a senior this year, Taylor. I'll be graduating in the spring and I'm in line for scholarships to some great universities. I can't have one stupid night messing that all up for me."

"Stupid night? Danielle died. Didn't you care about her at all?"

"We only went on a few dates—I didn't know she was a pill head." I sat up taller. He must have recognized my anger. He quickly added, "Yes, I liked her, but I thought we were just going to be drinking some beer at a campfire. I never dreamed Lindsey would show up with her Amish boyfriend and that other dude would appear out of nowhere." Now he turned hard eyes on me. "What the hell was that?"

I glanced around. No one was paying any attention to us. I whispered, "I'm sorry. I had no idea, either. Lindsey was just as freaked out as we were."

I closed my eyes and I was back in the dark woods.

"They're gone? What do you mean they left?"

I slunk back against Lindsey. The newcomer was average height, with a heavy-set frame. His brown hair was longish and messy. His eyes flashed darkly as his gaze passed over each of us in turn. He wore a leather jacket, but I noticed his pants were like Matthew's—homespun.

"Hey, look dude, we don't want any trouble. Your problem is with Jackson, not us," Hunter said.

"Yeah, Monroe, calm down. I'll get your money," Matthew said.

"This isn't a kiddie game." Monroe's hand slipped into his pocket and he pulled out a handgun. He aimed the gun at me. "I am going to shoot this little bitch if I don't get paid in one hour."

"Are you fucking kidding?" Hunter said. He stepped in front of me. "She didn't steal your drugs."

"That's right. She's an innocent little bird. But as I see it, the only way I'm going to get my money is to create a situation where the rest

of you have the incentive to go after it. If you decide to run off, abandoning the little bird, I'll put a bullet in her head." He sneered. "Oh, and I'll also leave a note in her pocket implicating each one of you." His smile was twisted and his eyes bright. "So, what's it going to be?"

The image cleared and I saw Hunter's face across from me. "We should have talked to the Sheriff a long time ago."

Hunter dropped his head back and groaned. "You're going to get into trouble you know that, don't you?"

My eyes began to blur with tears. I sniffed in the emotions and worked hard to keep my voice steady. "You were the one who reminded me how shallow it was to worry about getting into trouble when so many people are dead, Hunter—*dead.* Does it really matter if we get punished, or even if you lose a scholarship?"

Hunter's face went limp and he sighed. "Naw. I guess it really doesn't."

My cellphone went off. I didn't recognize the number. "Hello," I answered.

"Is this Taylor?" the female voice asked. It was familiar and I caught my breath.

"Yes, who is this?"

"Sarah. Is your car working?"

"Ah, yeah. The tow truck easily pulled it back onto the road last night and I drove home."

"We need to talk. Can you come to my Mam's house to pick me up? I'll tell her I need to get some craft supplies and you're going to drive me."

My mind swirled with the possibilities. It was still early enough that I could make the trip and be home by dark, like I'd promised my mom. "Sure, I'll come right out."

"Thanks, Taylor. See you soon."

I hung up and found Hunter staring at me. "You're not really going out there are you?"

"To the Amish community?" Yeah, why—what's the big deal?"

"That psycho was Amish. I don't think it's a good idea."

"I'm going to talk to a friend. I'll be fine." I asked the waitress to make my order to go and turned back to Hunter. "It might be a good idea for you to talk to your parents. It would be better if they heard everything from you, rather than the sheriff."

He looked resigned and I slid out of the booth.

"Hey, be careful," he said.

I offered him a curt nod and walked away as a chill passed over me.

I didn't like the idea of going back out to the community by myself, but curiosity about what Sarah had to say was stronger than any apprehension I felt.

I'd have time to visit Lindsey and get back home before dark. It would be nice to hang out with Mom for the evening, and with her problems with Dad, I think she needed it even more than I did.

14

The sun was setting beyond the snow-blanketed hills when we turned into the Swarey's farm. A small white house was nestled between a creek and a barn. Behind the house I could just make out the tin rooftops of several more barns. The property had a desolate, rambling feel. There were no children running around, and no dogs greeted us when we stepped out of the car. I was thankful for the brightness from the snow. It was hard to collect evidence in the dark.

"This place is a little forlorn," Toby commented. The Marshal's icy breath drifted out in front of him.

I zipped up my jacket and jogged up the steps to the front door. "There's no chimney smoke or lights on in the house. I don't think they're home."

"Where would they be on a bitter, snowy evening like this?"

I knocked several times and then gripped the porch railing, surveying the quiet farm. "No telling. The bishop has these secret meetings sometimes. You'd love it. They get together in dark barns to discuss the problems in the community—who's in trouble, what the punishment will be. I know firsthand about those and they're creepy as hell."

"Or maybe father and son are out doing some grocery shopping." Toby winked and I blew out a short laugh. "Either way, there's still a possibility they're doing something in one of these barns. It wouldn't be unreasonable to take a walk around, looking for them—would it?"

Toby's sly look made me hold in a smile. "I was thinking along the same lines. They'll probably show up in a few minutes anyway." I took the lead and the snow crunched under my boots. Toby pushed the barn door of the nearest building open just enough for us to slide in. The interior was dark, except for shards of moonlight coming in through the few windows and gaps between the boards. There was no electricity. I glanced at the lantern hanging on the peg near the entrance and ignored it. Removing my flashlight from my belt, I shined it ahead. A Bobcat was parked inside, along with a push-style lawn mower and several other pieces of farm equipment. A pile of dented, old gutters littered the one corner, and a table, covered with tools and a chainsaw, in the other. We silently crossed the dirt floor and paused at the next doorway out of the building.

"Clear?" Toby asked me.

"I'd say so," I replied. We left the building through the side doorway and aimed for the path that wound behind the house, toward a cluster of barns and sheds. The moon gave off enough brightness that I didn't need the flashlight. I pointed out the faint tracks we were following in the snow. Someone had walked back this way after it had stopped snowing.

We passed the broken structure of an old swing set and a

wall of round hay bales stacked alongside the hedgerow. The trail narrowed when we came to the first shed. Toby waited behind me as I followed the tracks to the door. I pushed it open and flashed my light inside. I was greeted with the sight of cobwebs and more farming tools. A thick layer of dust coated everything. The inside was small, and a quick look was all I needed to see it was empty.

"What exactly are you looking for, Sheriff?" Toby was waiting for me outside.

He was an easy man to work a case with. He didn't say too much, and when he did speak, it was usually something of substance. He had a pretty good sense of humor, and enjoyed the psychology of crime as much as I did.

I proceeded to the next shed and he followed. "I'm not really sure, but two women are missing, and this farm could possibly be the last place either one of them was seen." I tugged the door open and a cloud of warm, noxious fumes struck my face. I waved the air and took a step back. "Oh, my God, what is that smell?"

Todd chuckled and took the lead. "That is the lovely aroma of pig shit."

I walked behind him down a narrow corridor that ended with a metal gate. On the other side of the gate was a pen filled with swine. I tried not to take a deep breath and leaned around Toby to get a better view of the animals. I quickly counted nineteen of the huge, spotted beasts. The room was filled with the sounds of their grunting and squealing.

"How did you know?" I turned to Toby.

"We had pigs growing up. One year I even showed a sow I'd raised from a piglet. Won a blue ribbon at the fair and everything."

"Did she have a name?"

The corners of his mouth lifted. "I called her Bella." When I laughed, he added. "She was a mighty pretty pig."

"I didn't know you could have a pig as a pet."

Toby's expression darkened and his smile was gone. "You can't, really. We brought her home from the local fair, and that fall my father and brothers butchered her."

The look of disgust must have shown on my face. He quickly added, "The worst part was having to eat different forms of her for breakfast during that long winter."

"Are you pulling my leg?"

"Wish I was. That's how most pigs end up. I never showed one of Dad's pigs again after that—and I've never eaten bacon again, either."

My stomach rolled and I backed away from the gate. "This pen full of pigs reminds me of the Wizard of Oz. Remember how Dorothy fell into one and the farmhands rushed to carry her out of there?"

"Pigs are downright dangerous at times. Even though I grew to care about Bella, I'd had a few close calls with the other pigs. They can be aggressive, and when they reach weights of five hundred pounds or more, they're more than formidable. I recall another time when one of the sows became sick and got down in the pen. The other pigs attacked her and then ate her. My brothers and I discovered her remains the next morning. There was almost nothing left of her."

The high humidity, screeching noises, and terrible smell finally got to me. I covered my mouth and left the building. The blast of fresh air took the stench away. I breathed deeply and shook the thoughts of Bella the pig away with a jerk of my head.

I looked in the direction of the sound of bleating. A herd of wooly-looking sheep charged up to the fence. After the encounter with the angry pigs, the sudden appearance of the sheep made my heart race.

"What's wrong with them?" I glanced at Toby.

"It must be feeding time." He lifted his chin and I followed his gaze.

Nicolas Swarey stomped through the snow. He carried a lantern, and the tight frown on his face made me roll my shoulders back and brace for his temper.

15

TAYLOR

My heart dropped into my stomach when I saw the tall man walking straight at me. There was no way to keep it a secret that I'd been visiting the Amish community.

I pulled my knit cap down further on my head in an attempt to hide.

"Taylor, what are you doing here?" Daniel asked.

He stopped a few feet away and forced a smile, but his voice carried the edge of worry with it.

I decided to tell a little bit of the truth. "Sarah is my friend. I'm helping her pick out some craft supplies."

"Since when do you hang out with my niece?" He tilted his head.

I racked my mind for an answer. "The benefit dinner for the minister—what was his name?"

"James Hooley?"

"Yeah, that's him. Well, I was there with another friend, and she introduced me to Sarah. We got to talking and I found out she was your niece." He stood motionless, doubt creasing the lines on his face. "We just kind of hit it off," I said, trying to be convincing.

"Does Serenity know about your new friendship?"

I glanced away and stared at the cart speeding up the driveway. It was pulled by a fat black pony with a prancing trot. A cloud of breath spread out before the animal as it passed by.

"Hello, Uncle Daniel!" several small children called out at the same time. The driver couldn't have been more than twelve. She waved at me with her free hand while she slapped the reins with the other.

The horses were the part of being Amish I liked the most. I could only dream of a life where the main mode of transportation was either on the back of a horse or in a buggy being pulled by one.

"Ah, no. I haven't really had an opportunity to talk to her lately." I met his curious gaze. "She's kind of busy with the shooting and all."

Daniel's face dropped. "I'm sorry, kid. Serenity told me about what you went through. I can't even imagine what it was like."

His words gave me the opportunity I needed. "It's nice to come out here to visit Sarah. It's quieter and everyone isn't talking about the shootings."

Daniel nodded. "Sure, I understand. It's one of the things I miss about my time being Amish." He reached out and patted my shoulder. "Sarah's a sweet girl. I'm sure you will be great friends." His smile was hollow.

"Why are you here anyway? I thought you were shunned." I bit my tongue when Daniel's eyes widened.

Daniel recovered and offered a small nod. "That was a

long time ago. I guess time healed our relationship. My family has allowed me some contact, and like you, I enjoy coming out here, so I take it whenever I can." He gestured at an Amish man walking in our direction. "My brother-in-law needed help researching some building supplies online, so I gave him assistance. I get dinner out of the deal, so it's a win-win all around."

"Aunt Reni always talks about how great Amish cooking is."

"You should join us. I'm sure my sister would like to meet you."

I was about to accept the invitation when Sarah appeared. "If we're going to make it to the craft store before it closes, we need to leave now, Taylor." She looked at Daniel. "Nice to see you, Uncle Daniel."

"I get it, you girls have plans," Daniel said.

Sarah took my hand and aimed for my car. "Bye, Uncle Daniel."

"Be careful," he said.

I waved at him before I got into driver's seat. He waved back, but he wasn't smiling anymore.

"I don't think Daniel is happy we're hanging around together," I said.

"Turn left," she instructed. Once we were on the road, moving farther away from her home, she leaned back and loosened her knitted scarf. "Phew—that was a close one. I had no idea Uncle Daniel would show up today of all days. He hardly ever comes around." She shot a sympathetic look my way. "He's probably worried I'll get you into trouble."

"Why would he think that?"

He shrugged and pursed her lips. "From what I heard, he was pretty rebellious when he was a kid. Maybe he thinks

I'll follow in his footsteps. We've had a lot of bad things happen in our community lately. He might be worried for your safety."

My jaw clenched and I glanced sideways. Sarah wore a plain black coat over a hunter green dress. Her cheeks were rosy from the cold and a few wisps of dark hair had escaped from under her white cap. Her green eyes darted away, avoiding me. "Where exactly are we going?" I asked.

"It's a meeting of sorts—like an intervention, I guess you could say."

"An intervention?" I wondered where an Amish girl would have heard such a word. "For who?"

"You'll see."

I glanced out the window at the darkening sky. There was no way I'd be home by dark. I didn't want to break my promise to Sarah, but I also didn't like the sinking in my stomach. I barely knew Sarah, and here I was going to some random place with her for a reason I didn't even understand.

"I don't have a lot of time. I told my mom I would be home soon."

"Turn here," Sarah instructed.

"There isn't anything there," I argued.

"It's a tractor path." She pointed to a depression off of the road.

"It's covered with snow."

"It's just a dusting. You won't get stuck." She looked smugly back at me.

Fear screamed in my mind. "I thought you wanted to talk to me, Sarah. You should have told me you had other plans."

"I didn't think it was a big deal. Besides, this is important."

My car rolled over the snow slowly. There were some tracks

ahead that looked like they might be hoof prints, but there weren't any buggy wheel marks. I followed the tracks up to a wooden-sided barn that sat back in the middle of a cluster of trees. I parked, and before I had a chance to say anything else, Sarah jumped out of the car. I grabbed my cellphone and ran to catch up with her.

"Why are we at this old barn?" I caught her arm, pulling her to a stop.

She swung around, and her annoyed look made me sway backward. "You have to trust me, Taylor. It's important, and that's all I'm going to say."

A horse whinnied and I craned my neck to see past Sarah. Six horses stood in the snow, tied among the trees. They were all saddled and fuzzy. Steam rose from a brown one's nostrils when it whinnied.

Will had told me about a creepy barn in the woods where Aunt Reni had been held by a group of vigilante Amish when she was working on Naomi's murder investigation. Could this possibly be the same barn?

When Sarah tugged me to go with her, I planted my feet firmly. "I'm not going in there."

I struggled against the taller girl, but she held onto me with strong arms.

"Stop it, Taylor!" She shouted.

My heart pounded as adrenaline coursed through my veins. I kicked out and caught her in the shin. She yelped and loosened her hold. I lost my balance and fell backwards, landing in the snow. I ignored the wet chill on the side of my face and scrambled to my feet. I whirled around and crashed into someone.

I pounded my fists into his chest and screamed. Arms encircled me from behind.

"Quiet, Taylor, you're going to get us caught!" Sarah whispered fiercely into my ear.

Matthew put his hand over my mouth. "Stop it, no one's going to hurt you." He spied over my shoulder. "Damn. She's a feisty little thing."

"She's also the sheriff's niece." A male voice called out from somewhere behind me. "Let her go, Sarah! Now!"

Sarah released me and I stumbled forward, spreading my legs to keep from falling again. Matthew reached out to steady me, but I swiped his hand away. "What is wrong with you people? You're all crazy," I turned in a circle. Five boys who I didn't know approached slowly from the side of the barn. They all wore black knit hats and dark coats. Four kept their eyes downcast, but one left the group and strode up to me. His face was heavily freckled, and his light-colored eyes were bright with intelligence.

The stranger offered his hand and I ignored it. "I'm sorry about all this." His voice was rough. "It didn't have to happen this way. Sarah, what were you thinking, bringing her here?"

"She was there that night, Mervin. She knows everything," Sarah said.

Something clicked in my mind and I looked up. "Mervin Lapp—David Lapp's brother?"

His brows drew together. "Yes, it was my brother who shot and killed Naomi Beiler."

I searched my memories of conversations I'd had with Daniel and Aunt Reni about Mervin Lapp. "Aunt Reni always talked so well of you, and Daniel thinks of you like family. What is going on?"

"Daniel and your aunt are two of my favorite people." His words shook a little. "We need to talk and it's cold and getting dark out here. I promise no one is going to hurt you and you can leave whenever you want. We need your help. Please, just hear me out."

The moon hung over the trees, giving off a soft glow. I trembled beneath my coat as my gaze drifted over the six boys, and finally landed on Sarah. She wasn't angry anymore. She looked thoughtful. Something glistened in her eyes that made my heart slow down.

I pulled my cellphone out of my pocket and typed a message. I held up the phone. "I just wrote a text message to the sheriff. It says where I am and who I'm with. If any one of you do anything to freak me out, I'm going to send this message. All I have to do is hit *send*, and you won't have time to stop me. So, if you don't want the law out here, you better not mess with me."

Mervin snorted and then smiled. "You're a lot like Sheriff Serenity. You have my word that nothing bad will happen to you, but it's always good to have a backup plan."

He stepped aside and motioned for me to follow him. My muscles tightened and my mind shouted that I must be an idiot.

But I joined him anyway.

16

SERENITY

The Amish man held up the lantern and it illuminated his face. I hadn't seen Nicolas Swarey in a couple of months and the change in him was startling. His face was thin and drawn. There were dark circles beneath his puffy eyes.

"What are you doing snooping around on my property, Sheriff?" His voice was harsh.

I glanced at Toby, who was smirking, but remaining silent.

"Don't take that tone with me, Nicolas. I simply came out to ask you a few questions." I gestured to Toby. "This is US Marshal, Toby Bryant. After we knocked on your door, we heard the sound of an animal in distress. We followed the path to check out the disturbance and discovered the hogs. That's where the noise came from."

The air was icy and silent between us. I waited for my words to sink in.

Nicolas finally spoke. "What did you want to ask me?"

"Can we speak in your house? It's chilly outside." I inclined my head.

Without a word, he turned on his heels and I stretched my legs to follow him. I glanced over my shoulder and Toby had a sly expression on his face. The Marshal's amusement of the situation was annoying.

A few minutes later we were seated in the Swarey's kitchen beneath a dull gas light. The room was pale yellow and sparse. A few dishes littered the sink and nonperishable groceries lined the counter. It seemed Nicolas and his son didn't have time to put the cereal and cans of soup into the cupboards. It was almost as cold inside the home as it was outside. There weren't any signs of a woman's presence in sight.

A chill raced up my spine as I considered how the man sitting across from me had eliminated the very existence of his missing wife from the house. I studied him, wondering how a man could be so unemotional about the loss of his spouse.

"Have you heard from your wife?" I asked.

"Nope. Afraid not," he answered tersely.

I crossed my arms and held his gaze. "Where do you think she might be?"

His lips pinched. "I told you before, I don't know. Why your interest all of a sudden?"

"It's still an open file, Nicolas. When people go missing, we keep looking for them."

"I done told you already, that woman wasn't right in the head. She hated living by our ways and couldn't wait to escape when Monroe was old enough and not in need of her care any longer."

"Escape—what was she escaping from?" It was Toby who asked the question.

"Laundry, house chores, church services—who knows. She was a lazy woman." He grunted, casting a wolfish scowl at the lawman.

I had to take a deep breath to keep my cool. "A lot of women wouldn't be interested in living a lifestyle from the eighteen hundreds. I can understand her plight wholeheartedly."

Nicolas didn't respond. He sat in his chair with an angry face and stiff body.

"We asked you this before but perhaps you can clarify some of your previous answers." I pulled the small notebook from the inside pocket of my jacket and flipped it open. "You said that your wife didn't have any living family, except an aunt and a few cousins in California."

"That's correct," he replied, bobbing his head up and down.

"We contacted those family members at the end of summer and they said they hadn't heard from your wife in around seventeen years."

"That's right. When we got married, she turned away from her people." He scrunched up his face. "They were unholy— into drugs, alcohol, and dalliances. It was the best thing for her."

"Your own son was arrested for selling an illegal substance."

Nicolas' fist slammed onto the table. "He was corrupted by his evil mother and fell into sin. Now that she's gone, he's repented and changed his ways."

I shot Toby a look to silence him. I didn't want to tip Monroe's father off to the fact that his son was not only still dealing drugs, but had gotten into the harder stuff.

I ignored his little rant. "You also told us that your wife didn't have any friends on the outside." Our eyes met. "Do you still maintain that statement?"

Nicolas licked his lip and raised his eyes to the right, indicating a lie was coming. "She had no friends."

"Has anyone come here looking for your wife since she disappeared?" I asked.

"Other than you, no one."

I narrowed my gaze on him. He didn't flinch and stoically returned my stare.

There was no sign of breaking on his stony face. "All right. That's enough for now. Have a good night."

He dipped his head as we walked by him and out the front door. The chill immediately permeated my jacket. The door closed behind Toby.

In a low voice, he said, "He's lying about Charlene Noble."

"I know. Unless we find a witness or some evidence that she did indeed come here to see Swarey's wife, we have nothing on Nicolas."

"We should talk to some of the locals, Sheriff." Toby darted a sideways glance my way, with the corner of his mouth raised.

"You're enjoying this way too much, you know that?"

"Every crime investigation has its fascinating aspects. Working an Amish mystery is especially intriguing." His face brightened as we trudged through the snow. "They don't react or respond like the usual witnesses, victims or suspects. They have their own sense of authority and moral codes to guide them."

We reached the car and climbed in. I started the engine and put the heater blowing on high. "That's an understatement. They have no qualms with vigilante justice, and sometimes that's their downfall."

"I know you're going to be busy with the fallout from the school shootings, but we really need to begin talking to some of the neighbor's about Charlene Noble."

"Oh, I intend to get started right now."

It was priceless to see his brows shoot up. "At this late hour?"

"I have a dinner date with my fiancé and his family right up the road. Trust me, Daniel's sister knows what's going on with everyone in the community. If the Indianapolis woman did come through here, she would be aware of it."

He smiled crookedly. "I do believe my stomach's growling."

I laughed. "Yeah, I thought it might. Marshal Bryant, you're going to get a big dose of that intrigue you've been wishing for—and you're going to love the food."

"I'm much obliged, Sheriff."

17

TAYLOR

I paused beside the horse and reached out to pet its velvety nose. It pressed against my hand, its breath warming my face.

"That's Reckless. He's my horse," Matthew said. He released a heavy breath. "I don't fool around with drugs anymore. I just wanted you to know that."

His tone was deliberate, and his eyes tried to hold mine, but I ignored him and stretched my legs to catch up with Mervin Lapp. When Mervin disappeared into the blackness of the barn's doorway, I hesitated and Sarah nudged me.

"It's okay. No one's going to eat you," I glanced over my shoulder. Her teeth flashed.

I really wanted to punch her pretty face, but controlled myself. She was five inches taller than me and had six strong boys as backup. My mind reasoned that these kids that I barely knew weren't going to do horrible things to me. My heart thrummed madly against my ribcage as I stepped into the darkness.

When my eyes adjusted to the murky lighting, I discovered we were walking between bales of hay, before we entered a much larger room. My attention was immediately drawn to the spots in the walls that shards of moonlight were shooting through. They looked like bullet holes.

Mervin went to a lantern hanging from a beam. He lit it and a soft glow illuminated a small circle below it. Everyone crowded into the lighted space.

"You're probably wondering why you're here, Taylor," Mervin said.

I barked a half-suppressed laugh. "You could definitely say that. Aren't these secret barn meetings reserved for the adults?"

It was Sarah who answered me. "Usually, but we have our own system for solving problems."

Sarah stood on my left side and Matthew had taken up the place on the other side of me. He was close enough that his shoulder brushed mine. I refused to glance his way. Lindsey and Matthew had met when his work crew had constructed a new deck at her house. After the job was completed, he'd snuck off several times to see her, and I'd been there each time. On those occasions, he'd barely spoken a word to me. Although I thought I knew him a little bit, I didn't really know him at all—and neither did Lindsey.

"Are you familiar with Monroe Swarey?" Mervin crossed his arms. He seemed older than a teenager as he waited for my answer.

I shook my head and Matthew poked my arm. "The guy who was at the campsite with me that night."

My mouth rounded. "So he was Amish."

Matthew nodded.

"I kind of thought so, but that was the first time I'd ever seen him," I answered truthfully and then shuddered when a vision of my captor popped up in my mind.

Mervin glanced at the other guys and exhaled. "Monroe may be Amish, but he isn't one of us." I held my breath for him to continue. "We've all had our wild moments, and even Matthew has finally come around and left his reckless days behind. Monroe is a different story. His actions are dangerous to our people...and yours." He took a step closer and the others followed suit, tightening the circle. "Some things have been going on in the community—bad things—and Monroe is the heart of it all." He licked his lips. "Matthew came to me yesterday and told me something terrible that had happened a couple months ago. He wants our help, but in order for us to help him, you need to help us."

"I don't understand."

Matthew spoke up. "I like Lindsey a lot. She's a fun girl and all, but I realize I've made a mistake hanging around with her—"

I interrupted him. "You were more than hanging around with her," I snapped.

Sarah hid a smile behind her hand and then looked at the ground.

"Yeah, well, it was a mistake. Setting up the meeting between Monroe and your friend, Jackson, was the worst mistake of all."

"Jackson was never my friend," I hissed. "You assume all non-Amish kids know each other—well, we don't. The only reason I was there that night was for Lindsey, because she wanted to see *you*."

Matthew's face reddened. He was about to reply when

Mervin cut him off with a hand thrust. "That part doesn't matter. What we need to know is how Jackson knew about Monroe in the first place."

"I have no idea. Like I said, I didn't really know Jackson at all." A memory teased my mind. I dug my boot toe into the dirt floor and glanced around. The other boys hadn't said a thing. It seemed like Mervin was taking the role as junior bishop, so I settled my gaze on him. "Maybe it was Danielle?"

"The girl who died?" Mervin's face took on the tightness of expectancy, making me swallow down the spit that pooled in my mouth.

"She overdosed on the crap she got from Monroe." I searched my memories. "She worked part-time at the gas station at the end of Burkey Road. I've seen buggies there before."

Mervin nodded, his gaze looking off into nothingness before it returned to me. "That makes sense. He meets up with people there."

"Why do you care so much about what he's doing? Shouldn't your elders be taking care of him?" I said.

A ghost of a smile toyed with his lips. "Oh, they will—but Monroe is pretty sly. We need proof, and we have to hurry before someone else is hurt."

"So, you're all playing detectives?" I looked around. Some pairs of eyes continued to stare back, except one boy, and Sarah, who glanced away. "That's crazy. You should talk to my aunt. She'll take care of all of this." When they remained stubbornly silent, I persisted. "Drug dealers are ruthless. He's just some Amish kid. Who knows what kind of dangerous person he's getting the stuff from?" I frowned at Mervin, as he was their leader. If I could convince him, the others would follow suit. "You're worried about someone else? Well, if you don't go to the authorities, you'll be the one getting hurt—or worse."

"Why didn't you talk to the sheriff about that night?" Mervin suddenly reminded me of an arrogant fox, looking at me with distaste.

I shifted between my feet. "At the time it didn't seem important."

"A girl died. Isn't that important enough?" Mervin said in steely voice.

Tears flooded my eyes and I dabbed at them.

Sarah pressed closer to me and touched my arm. "Leave her alone, Mervin. You don't have to be mean."

"I'm only speaking the truth." He raised his voice. "We're all at fault. We all knew what Monroe was up to, but we kept quiet, more intent on protecting our own backsides, and keeping the elders' focus away from us, than taking the risk of talking to them"—he looked at me—"or the sheriff about our fears. It's too late for this Danielle girl, but we can still right our wrongs."

"What do you want from me?" I asked through wet lips.

"You have to tell us exactly what happened the night Danielle died. The entire truth."

I glanced at Matthew and he offered me a sympathetic look and a slow nod.

I rubbed my hands into my temples and took a deep breath, knowing I should have done this a long time ago.

I forced the words out of my mouth. "I thought I was going to die..."

18

SERENITY

The kitchen was too hot. I unzipped my jacket and slid it off, hanging it on the back of the chair. I glanced at Daniel. He was listening to his brother-in-law talk about the benefits of weaning calves early, but the firm set to his jaw told me he wasn't paying much attention to the farmer's ramblings. Toby sat on the other side of me and my gaze drifted his way. He eyed me with his usual crooked smile. He seemed to be enjoying the dinner in the Amish household immensely. He had accepted seconds on his plate, and had already asked several nosey questions about the Amish lifestyle. He seemed oblivious that he'd raised the hackles on my fiancé's back several times. Daniel was a jealous man, and Toby was the kind of guy who enjoyed pushing people's buttons. The Marshal's innocent look wasn't deceiving, though. I would bet he knew exactly the pot he had stirred up by being at my side when we arrived at Rebecca's house.

"It is so sad what happened at the town's school the other day." Rebecca's eyes glistened. "I cannot imagine such a thing. Why did that boy kill his classmates and teachers, Serenity?"

I cleared my throat. "I'm trying to figure that out, but it won't be easy, since the shooter is dead. He's the only one who can tell us for sure why he did it." Everyone became silent around the table. Daniel's eyes met mine and I folded my hands neatly on the table. "We can gather evidence and make an educated guess."

"Those poor families. It seems worse that it happened in a place where the children should have been safe and protected." Rebecca stirred her cup of tea, the heat rising from it mingled with the other cooking smells in the kitchen.

"It's a horrible tragedy," Daniel spoke up. His eyes were like dark pools as he stared at me. "Did the evidence lead you to the Amish?"

My gaze whipped to Daniel. "What do you mean?"

"Reuben said when he was on his way back from the feed mill, he saw your vehicle parked at the Swarey's place." Daniel's handsome face was set in stone, emotionless.

I glanced at Rebecca's husband. The man had a long black beard and dull brown eyes. He'd always struck me as a man with no curiosity. Perhaps I was wrong about that.

My blood bubbled. I wasn't happy that Daniel brought this up in the presence of his sister and brother-in-law, but maybe I could use it to my advantage.

I turned to Rebecca. "How well did you know Nicolas' wife?"

"Are you barking up *that* tree again?" Reuben thrust his chest out. "That woman wasn't one of us. It was a mistake that Nicolas married her. After all these years, she finally realized it and ran off to live among the English."

I leaned forward, keeping my gaze locked on Reuben's defiant face. "The problem is she *isn't* living among the English.

As far as I can tell, Erin Swarey disappeared into thin air." My voice grew louder. "A missing person is of interest to me."

Reuben's shoulders lowered and he pushed his mashed potatoes around with his fork. My focus switched to Rebecca. "I apologize for bringing up a case over dinner, but it's important. I'll ask you once again—what was your relationship with Nicolas' wife?"

Rebecca looked at her husband, and when he didn't raise his head, she licked her lips and began talking. "Erin was a friend. She had a generous spirit and was always kind to me and the other women. We understood how difficult it was for her to overcome her ties to the English world, and we helped her as much as we could. She tried really hard in the early years she was among us, when Monroe was a small child. She cooked and cleaned the house as well as any of us." She smiled faintly, staring past me. "I recall a time right after I had my second baby. It was a difficult delivery and I was constrained to the bed for almost a week, recovering. The other women in the community brought dinners for my family and helped clean the house and care for the baby, but what Erin did got me through the ordeal more than anything anyone else provided." Her eyes met mine again. "She brought a book everyday—it was a historical story about a family living in Ireland and the trials they went through to come to America. She read to me for several hours each day, even making different sounds for the voices. Erin had a wonderful spirit and I was fond of her." She frowned. "As the years passed and Monroe grew older, Erin began to withdraw from the community, and even from me. The light left her eyes. She wasn't happy anymore."

The kitchen was quiet, except for the rustling of the kids at the end of the table.

"Children, you're excused," Reuben said flatly.

With a flurry of movement Daniels' nephews were out of their chairs and running through the doorway. His nieces took their time rising and began gathering the dinner plates.

"Out with you, too." Reuben flapped his hands, encouraging the girls to leave the room. They glanced at each other in surprise, but didn't hang around to argue with their father. Once they were released from their usual chores, they were gone as quickly as the boys were.

I recognized the little blonde girl. Her name was Christina and I'd saved her life about a year earlier. I had performed CPR on her after she'd fallen into a flooded ditch. A few months later she'd nearly died again, when she'd ingested poisonous water hemlock. The child was only six or seven years old, and yet she was already a well-trained little Amish girl. And then I remembered Daniel's oldest niece.

"Where's Sarah?" I asked Rebecca.

Her face brightened. "Taylor took her to the craft store to get some supplies." The spoon that I was about to scoop up the last bite of coleslaw froze in midair, and Rebecca's eyes widened. "Did you not know they are friends?"

"Uh, no, I wasn't aware of that." I shot a questioning look at Daniel and he shrugged. "I have been busy lately."

Thick silence hung in the kitchen and Reuben bolted up. "Daniel, why don't I show you our new Hereford calves. They're a fine lot."

Toby stood up and said, "I'd like to see them too, if you don't mind me tagging along."

Toby was a smooth operator. He realized that I would get further with Rebecca if the men weren't around. Daniel was more reluctant to leave.

"Why don't you go see the cows—I'll help Rebecca get the kitchen cleaned up," I coaxed, hoping I'd disguised any tone of begging from my voice.

Daniel gave me the—we-have-a-lot-to-discuss-later look before he joined Reuben and Toby and left the room. The door closed, and I was finally alone with Rebecca in the empty kitchen. She carried the plates to the sink and I joined her with an armful of glasses.

"What do you think changed for Erin?" Caution flicked in Rebecca's eyes, and I hurried on, "Why did she become depressed?"

Rebecca set the dishes into the sink and faced me. "Nicolas is not a good man. He put on an act for a while, pretended to be something he was not while their marriage was young and Monroe was just a child. Over time, his true nature began to shine through."

"What did he do?" I asked.

Rebecca gazed around the room, making sure the coast was clear. Even though we were quite alone, she still whispered. "Nicolas was always a violent man, even when he was a teenager. He hid that side of himself when he courted Erin. She chose to join our people because he convinced her to. He made her feel safe and secure with him." She stared at the sudsy water while she spoke. "I remember the first time she showed me the bruising. He was careful to only touch her below the neck, so no one else would be the wiser."

My face flushed with heat and my fists balled. "Didn't you report the abuse to the bishop?"

Her eyes went wide. "Oh, yes. I told Reuben about it, and he went to the elders. Nicolas denied it all, said his wife was injured by a horse or fell from a ladder while cleaning cobwebs.

He accused Erin of having emotional problems, and since she used to be English, the bishop and ministers were reluctant to believe her side of things. They counseled Erin to be an obedient wife." Rebecca's voice cracked and a tear slipped down her cheek. "The other women began spending less time with Erin, and even I cut back my contact with her after Reuben advised me to do so."

"Why would Reuben care if you hung out with her?"

Her attention went to the dishes again. "Nicolas had insinuated that Erin was a woman who stirred up trouble. Reuben didn't want me getting entangled in whatever problems she was having."

"So when your friend needed you most, you let her down?" I didn't try to hide my disgust.

Rebecca stiffened. "I am very sorry for abandoning her, but if I wanted to have a healthy marriage with my own husband, I had to follow his guidance." I threw the dish towel onto the counter, and she rushed out, "It's our way, Serenity. I see it's hard for you to understand, but it's what I chose and am content with."

"Your lifestyle isn't my concern—Erin Swarey is. Do you have any idea where she might have gone?"

Rebecca shook her head. "She never said a word to me about leaving."

"What about a friend of hers—an English woman she might have been in contact with? Did someone come to visit her in the days leading up to her disappearance?"

"No, I didn't see anyone or hear about such a visit." Rebecca looked at me with clear, unflinching eyes. She was being truthful.

A loud knock on the door startled us both. Rebecca crossed

the floor and opened the door. Bishop Esch strode into the kitchen, bringing with him a blast of wintry air.

"Where is your husband, Rebecca?" His gaze traveled around the room until he noticed me. "Sheriff, I wondered if that was your car out there. I'm surprised to see you in our neck of the woods. I would have guessed your services would be needed in town with the tragedy there."

I leaned back against the counter. "Nice to see you too."

He tipped his hat and then returned his attention to Rebecca. "I must see Reuben"

"You'll find him in the cattle barn," Rebecca said.

After the bishop was gone, Rebecca plopped down on the nearest chair and rubbed her face. "I hope nothing is amiss."

"You weren't expecting Aaron this evening?"

"Oh, no. I worry when he shows up after dark unannounced."

I recalled the bishop's overly brisk manner and had to agree with her. He was on a mission that either meant something was wrong or someone was in deep trouble.

I gathered up my jacket and car keys. "Thanks for dinner. It was delicious as always, but I really need to get back to town. I have a stack of paperwork to get through before morning."

She rose and blocked my way. The look on her face made me think she'd bitten into something sour.

"Daniel mentioned your wedding earlier. He's hoping we'll be able to attend." She swallowed a gulp. "We would love to be there, but I'm not sure if it will be allowed."

"Who do you expect permission from?" I dared to ask.

"It's up to the bishop, and since Moses is a minister and Daniel's father, he has a say also. You understand how shunning works, right?"

I nodded and forced my face to remain neutral.

"Because Daniel was shunned, going to his wedding is usually against our rules. We're hoping an exception can be made for you."

"Me?"

"Of course! You've done so much for our community, keeping us safe and solving our crimes. That is all being discussed, I'm sure."

I smiled politely. I had to respect their culture even though I didn't always like it.

"It would make us both very happy if you're there, but I understand if it doesn't happen."

The slap of the wind on my face when I stepped outside helped clear my head. A dim light flickered in one of the barn windows and several cows mooed. The moon was high in the sky, its light shined down. The icy snow crunched beneath my feet when I crossed the yard to my car. I'd send Toby a text to get his butt down here so we could head back to town.

I was dreading any conversation with Daniel. It wasn't just because of his paranoia about Toby assisting me on the case. I was more frustrated by the discussion with Rebecca about the Amish notion of married life and wives obeying husbands, and the fact that Daniel's family probably wouldn't even attend our wedding. The entire situation was annoying and depressing.

"Sheriff Serenity?" a small voice called out from the darkness.

I followed the sound and came upon red-cheeked Christina standing beneath a pine tree. She wore a fluffy knit cap and a thick black coat. The toes of her black boots poked out from under her blue dress.

"What are you doing out here? It's cold." I rubbed my hands together.

The little girl curled her finger, motioning me to duck under the tree's branches. I did and bent down.

"What's this all about?"

"I heard you talking to Mama. I shouldn't have been listening—it was an accident." Her voice came out stilted, as if she hadn't mastered the English language yet.

I smiled. The child was precocious. "It's okay. That happens to me all the time."

She blew out an icy breath. "I was with the Yoders one day, and we stopped at the gas station's store to pick up some snacks." She lifted her chin. "I was spending the night with Barbara, and her Mama wanted us to have something salty to eat, 'cause she said her cabinets were bare." I nodded, urging her on. "Well, I saw Mrs. Swarey that time—"

I interrupted. "Erin Swarey, Monroe's mom?"

She nodded vigorously. "It was her, and she was with a woman I didn't know."

"Was the woman Amish?"

She shook her head. "No. She was English. She had ugly arms." My brow furrowed, and she said, "There were weird drawings on her arm, like a funny looking tree and a heart. That's why I stared at her when I walked by to use the restroom. They were sitting at one of the tables. When I came close, they stopped talking."

I held my breath. "When do you think this was?"

The girl shrugged. She appeared to become distracted by the bishop's horse that was tied to the hitching rail, stomping his hoof.

"Christina, listen to me. This is very, very important. Can you remember what the weather was like that day?"

"It was hot outside. I remember I was sorry I wore my apron and I was sweating. I was going to Barbara's for her birthday, too."

"When is Barbara's birthday," I asked.

The child looked up, thinking hard. "In August, I think."

My toes felt like tiny needles were pricking them and the girl's nose was beginning to run. "Is there anything else you recall about Mrs. Swarey and her friend? Anything at all?"

"Only that they both looked sad," Christina said.

I absorbed the information and straightened. "Thanks for talking to me. That was very brave and smart of you."

The girl's cold little face beamed up at me.

"Go on and get inside before you turn into an ice cube." She giggled and I shooed her toward the front door.

I pivoted before I reached my car and stretched my legs up the hill. The bishop's distracted avoidance of me hadn't slipped my notice. The man was up to something, and I wasn't leaving until I found out what it was.

19

TAYLOR

The barn walls faded and the chill disappeared. I was back in the woods, alone with the stranger.

The guy circled me and flicked the gun left and right as he spoke. "Are you afraid?"

I struggled to take a breath. My heart was hammering so loudly I was sure he could hear it. "I would be stupid if I wasn't."

He laughed. "Yeah, I guess that's right." He eyed me up and down. "You haven't been drinking, have you?"

I shook my head, glad I didn't have to speak to answer the drug dealer.

"That's smart, real smart. It's always best to have your wits." He eased back against a tree as if he was suddenly bored with me. "I make a living selling dope, but I never use the stuff. I don't drink alcohol, either." He taped the side of his head. "I always have to be one step ahead of everyone else."

His relaxed posture settled my nerves a little bit. "Are you Amish?"

My question caught him off guard. He tilted his head. "Why, you are a clever girl. What makes you think I'm Amish?"

"Your pants," I said.

He laughed again. "Nice observation. If I were Amish it would be easier to change quickly if I only had my t-shirt to swap out. Don't you agree?"

We stared at each other and he was the first to look away. "It would be a shame if your friends don't show up to save you. I think I might even feel bad about blowing your brains out."

The sound of leaves rustling reached my ears, and I searched the woods with squinted eyes. The noise grew louder and the stranger straightened up, stepping away from the tree. When Hunter bounded into the clearing he nearly bumped into me. Matthew and Lindsey were right behind him.

"She's dead! My God, she's dead," Hunter shouted. His eyes were wet and wild.

Lindsey grabbed my arm. "It's true. We found Danielle in her pickup truck. There was foam on her mouth and she wasn't breathing."

"Are you sure she was dead—where was Jackson?" The drug dealer's face was wide with excitement.

Matthew bent over to catch his breath and Hunter sunk to his knees, clutching the sides of his face.

"I touched her cheek and it was ice cold—she's dead," Lindsey said.

Matthew straightened up. "We didn't see Jackson. He's gone."

The stranger sighed and held up the gun, backing away. "If any one of you open your mouths about what happened here, I will find you and kill you." His smiled deepened. "I won't just snuff your lives out, I'll go after the people you love, too. You got that?" he threatened.

Everyone nodded, except me. "You don't want your money now?"

Lindsey dug her elbow into my side, but I ignored her, meeting the stranger's startled gaze.

"It's your lucky day, smart girl. This news is payment enough."

I blinked and was back inside the cold, dark barn with the small group of Amish kids again. I had talked while I had remembered. The little bit of light emitting from the lantern cast shadows across everyone's faces, but one thing I could see clearly is that they were all riveted by my story.

"Your friend, Monroe, took off into the trees and I never saw him again. The rest of us made a pact to keep that night a secret. We were more afraid for the lives of those we loved than anything else." I crossed my arms and squeezed, wishing I was home in my bed.

Sarah patted my back. "It's all right. We understand. Monroe is scary sometimes, and he might just follow through with his threat."

"He would. I'm convinced of that," Mervin said. He turned to Matthew. "Then what you said is true, and we have an English girl, the Sheriff's niece, to back your story up."

"Do you hear that?" Matthew asked. He walked away from the circle and paused.

"What?" I whispered, the word quivering from my lips.

Sarah hooked her arm around my shoulder and I didn't move away. We trembled side by side, while we all strained to hear something.

"I think we better end our gathering," Mervin suggested.

"What, before I've had a chance to speak?" a voice boomed out from the shadow in the corner.

Had he been hiding there the entire time? Did he hear what I said? I clenched my teeth.

Monroe swaggered into the light. He grinned at me and pulled back his coat flap, exposing his revolver for everyone to see.

Anger swelled up inside of me. Jackson might have gone on a murderous rampage because of this sadistic jerk.

"What is your problem? Just go away—no one invited you," I shouted, moving forward.

Mervin's hand caught my shoulder and stopped my momentum.

"Brave and bright," Monroe drawled. "I'm really starting to like you."

"Answer her question, Monroe," Mervin called out. "You aren't welcome here, and you know it."

"That's never stopped me before. Don't you remember when you all"—he spread his arm wide—"would skip over me when you made the ball teams?" The circle broke as everyone stepped back. "Of course, that was a blessing in disguise. I was able to just pick the team I thought would win and jump in." His smile was twisted. "No one had the guts to stop me. Isn't this kind of the same thing? None of you are going to do anything about the loser English girl ODing, and none of you are going to keep me from continuing to sell my wares, either."

"A girl died," Matthew said limply.

"So what? Do you think I care about her? She meant nothing to me." His gaze shifted my way. "Unlike this little English girl who refrained from drinking or doing any drugs that night, the other girl partied and paid the price for it. I'm only providing a product that some people want. The rest of you can go back to your safe little worlds, knowing that as long as you stay out of my way, nothing will happen to any of you."

"What are you, judge, jury, and executioner?" I asked.

Monroe made a funny face. "I never thought of it that way." He shrugged. "Maybe I am."

Mervin extended his arm. "We used to be friends, Monroe—a long time ago. I only want to help you before it's too late."

"Too late?" He grunted. "I'm just getting started."

"The elders will find out and maybe even the Sheriff. You're destroying our community with the poison you're bringing into it," Mervin said.

Monroe walked up to Mervin. "You have no authority over me."

"But they do," Mervin said quietly.

I strained to hear. *Clip clops* on the pavement were getting louder.

Monroe heard them and looked around at the group wildly. "I have it all written down, and if you talk, then I'll start talking. Like how you have your driver buy you beer, Elmer. Or how about you, Sam—you've been sneaking off with your girlfriend and doing the wild thing in the storage shed behind the schoolhouse." He pointed his finger at Sarah. "Then there are the girls and their makeup and radio parties in your barn when your parents are away." He chuckled at the look of horror on Sarah's face.

"None of those things are as bad as what you've been up to, Monroe," Mervin said confidently.

Monroe made a *tsk tsk* sound as he slipped back into the shadows. "I wager your allied front is breaking…" And he was gone.

As the sound of approaching buggies grew louder, three of the boys darted out the door. A moment later, the sound of a whinny and pounding hooves shook the night.

Matthew implored Mervin, "We've got to go. If they find out we're meeting up like this at night—in a barn with girls—it will be over for us."

"Save yourself, Matt. I'm not abandoning the girls," Mervin replied calmly.

Matthew turned to leave and stopped. "Dammit," he cursed.

"What's going to happen to you?" I asked Sarah.

A tenuous smile tugged at the corners of her mouth. "We're going to find out—together."

The barn door burst open, and the bishop appeared in the doorway. He was tall and thin. His white beard and hair shone brightly as he aimed a flashlight our way. Sarah gripped my hand tightly. Mervin and Matthew moved in closer.

Next through the doorway was Sarah's father, followed by several more dark cloaked, bearded men.

I spotted Daniel and my heart sank into my stomach, but I really wasn't prepared for Aunt Reni to come bursting through the door with her gun poised in front of her.

"Oh, no," I muttered. "No, no, no."

My aunt flashed her light around the barn before she lowered her weapon and approached me.

She stared at me with a cold look that made my knees week. "You have a lot of explaining to do," she said.

20

SERENITY

"I want to talk to these boys." I stared at Aaron Esch with narrowed eyes and my jaw set.

The bishop chuckled as he smoothed his snowy colored beard down with his hand. "I'm afraid this is community business." His bushy brows arched. "Unless there's another reason you're here, Sheriff, and you're not being truthful with me."

The old man always made me squirm a little bit and I hated the feeling. He was a master at subtle intimidation. Although he'd never attended a university or even received an education past eighth grade, he was one sharp cookie.

My gaze drifted over to the small group of teenagers gathered under the one dim lantern in the center of the barn. Taylor stood close to Daniel's side, and Toby and Reuben were quietly talking to the boys.

When I looked back at the bishop, I was calmer. No one was injured. I would find out more from my niece than any of the Amish anyway.

I lowered my voice. "Taylor is my niece, and I'm not happy to discover her in this same barn that your men held me captive in last year."

"You're quite mistaken if you think I'm happy to find the girl here. When our children mingle with outsiders, nothing good ever comes from it," he said.

"For once we agree, but I'm going to get to the bottom of this, Aaron. Don't be surprised if you see me in the next few days."

"I would expect just that," the bishop said. He touched the brim of his hat and strode away.

Daniel guided Taylor over to me. I searched her face and saw only fear there.

"Are you cold?" I asked her.

She nodded, averting her gaze.

"Daniel, please take her to my car. I've got this covered."

His mouth twitched. "I see. Will you be coming home anytime soon?"

I paused to think. "I have to stop by the office. Toby and I are meeting with Bobby and Todd." A thought occurred to me, and I cringed inwardly when I added, "Do you mind dropping Toby off at the department before you go on home? I want to talk to my niece alone."

A tight smile spread on his lips. "Do I really have a choice?" He rolled his eyes. "Sure thing."

Reuben caught up with Daniel and whispered something to him. He motioned for his daughter to follow.

Toby lingered by my side. "Does this have anything to do with the Swarey situation?"

I eyed the Marshal. He was either grasping at straws or very perceptive. I was betting it was the latter.

"That's what I'm going to find out. I have my suspicions, though." I leaned in. "Why don't you try to pull up a picture of Charlene Noble—maybe something from social media."

He twirled the end of his Doc Holiday style mustache. "Did your private talk with Rebecca shed any light on her disappearance?"

"Naw, not at all. But her little girl saw a woman with Erin Swarey at the gas station at the edge of the community."

"Really?" He drew the word out slowly. "Then we might have a witness that Charlene was in Blood Rock. This tale is getting more interesting by the minute."

"A six-year-old's memory isn't going to hold a lot of weight in court, but it's a start. If she remembers Charlene, then someone else might, too."

Toby turned to leave, and then paused. "The kid won't be blabbing that information, will she?"

I shook my head. "Amish kids are good at keeping secrets. I don't expect her to—why?"

"Seems to me if someone did something to make Charlene Noble disappear, that person wouldn't want anyone confirming that the woman was indeed in the community around the time of her disappearance."

Icy tentacles gripped my heart. "Got it." I pulled my cellphone out. I wasn't taking any chances with Christina's life. I'd have an officer patrol the neighborhood until I found out what really happened to Erin Swarey—and her friend, Charlene Noble.

21

TAYLOR

I sat in Aunt Reni's car and watched Sarah climb into Daniel's jeep. Warm air blew from the vents into my face, and I rocked my head back and shut my eyes. Images of carnage in the school's hallway assailed my mind, but instead of trying to banish them this time, I studied each and every victim I passed by in a morbid way. There were puddles of blood everywhere. I nearly slipped in one and jumped another. Book bags that had been dropped here and there made the obstacle course even more difficult. The bodies were the worst. Some lay unmoving, frozen and staring, while some hands twitched and a few heads rolled back and forth.

The sounds of groans and crying banged inside my head, and I pressed my hands to my ears.

"Taylor, snap out of it."

I popped my eyes open and Aunt Reni's hand gripped my arm. Her eyes were wide, peppered with worry.

"What?" I muttered. My head was heavy and my mind was slow.

She snapped her fingers and reached over to pull me into a tight hug. "It's okay—you're safe."

I didn't realize I'd been swaying back and forth in my seat until Aunt Reni stopped my movement. Her grip was strong and she smelled like vanilla. I buried my face into her soft hair and let the tears roll down my cheeks.

"It's all my fault. I could have stopped Jackson." I gulped and stuttered. "If...if only I'd told you about that night. I'm so sorry...sorry."

"Shh, it's okay. Let it all out." Aunt Reni rubbed my back and didn't let go when I tried to pull away. "It's all a part of the healing process."

The sound of Daniel's engine and the pounding of hooves on pavement had faded away into nothingness by the time I opened my eyes. We were parked alongside the barn and all alone. Everyone else had already left. Moonlight sprayed down through the trees, casting an eerie glow on the wooden boards.

I sucked in a hot breath and my rubbed my eyes. Aunt Reni finally released her hold and I sat back. My throat shook, but I managed to speak. "Where did your friend—the Marshal—go?" My mind was fuzzy with the events leading up to my breakdown in the car.

"He left with Daniel, so I could speak with you alone. Daniel also gave Sarah a ride. The rest of the boys returned home with their horses."

Her voice was easy. There was no trace of anger there.

I looked up and blinked. "Was the bishop mad?" I couldn't help but shudder when I pictured his tall, stoic frame striding into the barn.

"He wasn't happy." She blew out and shook her head. "At

least he decided not to deal with the boys and Sarah at that moment. Their day of reckoning will arrive soon enough."

"Just because they met up in a barn?" I wiped off my cheeks with the back of my hand and glanced at the vehicle's clock. "It's only eight o'clock."

Aunt Reni grunted. "For those kids, it's late enough. Sneaking off for a secret meeting with a couple of girls—one being an Englisher—is sure to get them into a lot of trouble."

"They're just doing what their elders do."

"Sure enough," she said, sighing.

The inside of the cab was quiet and warm, and I my head began to clear.

"Do you want to talk about it?" Aunt Reni asked carefully.

I glanced over and nodded. I took a deep breath and pushed the air out slowly. "I should have talked to you sooner." I swallowed the lump down in my throat. "Everyone would still be alive."

"That's not necessarily true, Taylor. Jackson was a messed-up kid with a vendetta, but he had no prior record or strange behavior that would have made authorities think he had the propensity to become a mass murderer. He kept it all hidden inside and then he snapped. You're lucky you survived, and you're not to blame for his horrific actions."

I wanted her to be upset with me, but her entire demeanor was way too understanding. I raised my voice. "Don't you want to know what happened?"

The corner of her mouth turned down in a slight frown. "Of course I do, but I want to make sure you're in the right state of mind to talk. I let your mom know you're with me. She's pretty upset."

I slumped in the seat. "What did she say?"

"Just that she wants me to get to the bottom of this. She asked me to help you."

"You can't help me, Aunt Reni. Not unless you can turn back time."

Her brow knitted. "Oh, many times have I wished that! I get where you're coming from, kiddo. I've been there, you know—like at the Coblenz wedding last summer. I arrived there too late to save the bride, groom, and several other family members. I replay it over and over in my mind, wondering if I'd realized the identity of the killer and how dangerous he was sooner, maybe I could have arrested him before he gunned down those people. And what about the Amish girls who were mutilated? If I'd been on the ball, perhaps I could have saved them, too." She stared out the window into the night. "Then there was the girl I shot dead. I thought she was pulling a weapon on my partner—she'd been involved in a violent burglary that same day. There are so many what ifs. I have trouble sleeping most nights, thinking about the innocent people I could've—should've—saved."

"It's not your fault! You try harder than anyone else to solve crimes. You've saved so many with your quick thinking and bravery. How can you even think that?" I scolded.

She smiled sadly. "It's my job. I'm responsible for people's lives. I'm the sheriff of Blood Rock. If you can blame yourself for the school massacre, then I must be guilty of the deaths of countless more lives."

"That's not true, Aunt Reni. You can't stop all the bad people from doing evil things."

"Bingo. For a sixteen-year-old, you're a lot wiser than most adults." She gave me a knowing look. "That's why you can't wrack yourself with guilt for what Jackson Merritt did." Tears welled in my eyes. "What were you doing out here tonight? Daniel mentioned you and Sarah had become friends and were going to a craft shop. Was there any truth to that?"

"That's what I thought we were doing. She called me out of the blue and asked if I'd drive her. I didn't really consider her a friend yet—just a girl I'd met and liked. I thought we might eventually grow to be friends."

"I see. It's sometimes difficult to be their friends. Our cultures are so different."

"Yeah, no kidding." My heart began hammering again, and I rushed out the words before I lost my nerve. "Sarah brought me here instead. I was upset with her for deceiving me. I had no idea the boys would come."

Aunt Reni's brow rose. "What was the purpose of their meeting?"

My aunt was pretty slick. She'd calmed me down and convinced me that the school shooting wasn't my fault, and now she was casually playing detective. But I didn't care; I had to tell her everything.

"They're worried about another teenager in their community—a bad kid, someone who has been causing all kinds of trouble." I met her intense gaze. "They wanted to hear my version of the events, to see if Matthew was telling them the truth..."

I wrapped my arms around my body and told Aunt Reni about the night in the woods—about Danielle's overdose and the drug dealer threatening me. I was careful not to leave anything out. When I was done talking, it felt like a heavy weight was lifted from my shoulders. For the first time in over two months, I was free.

Aunt Reni tapped the steering wheel and then put her car

in reverse. She backed around and pulled up alongside my car. "I'm going to follow you home, Taylor. I have to get back to the office, so I won't be able to go in and chat with your mom." I hesitated and then nodded. "You have to be a big girl and tell her exactly what you told me. She's your biggest advocate, and she'll understand. She'll know just what to say to make you feel better."

"Are you mad at me?" I ventured.

"Of course not. You were in the wrong place at the wrong time. It happens to a lot to teenagers." She turned a harder look on me. "But you have to start being smarter, making your own decisions about what's best for you, instead of following your friends' leads. I know you were trying to be a good pal to Lindsey, but when those little warning bells go off in your head in the future, you have to heed them. Trust your instincts and you'll be all right."

"Thank you," I mumbled, feeling the tears pool in my eyes.

"It's okay to cry. You've been through a hell of a lot—seen atrocious things most people never face. It's going to be a while before things are back to normal. That's just the way it is."

"How can anything ever be normal again?"

"Because life goes on for the living. Your spirit is strong and you will recover from this. Don't get me wrong, you'll never forget what you saw in that school or what happened to you in the woods. The pain and harshness of it all will fade in time so that it's more like a bad dream, but don't lock up your emotions inside. Talk to your parents, your brother, your friends, and of course, me, as much as you need to. Talking is the best way to deal with it."

"I will." I pulled the handle and pushed open the door. Cold wind rushed into my face.

"Taylor?" I looked over my shoulder at Aunt Reni. "Do you know the name of the Amish boy who sold Danielle the drugs and pulled the gun on you?"

"Monroe Swarey."

The winter wind was no match for the chilling look on my aunt's face. If I didn't hate him so much, I would have felt sorry for the kid.

22

SERENITY

"You don't have enough evidence that a crime was committed at the Swarey farm to get the judge to issue a search warrant," Todd argued.

He sat in one of the chairs across from my desk. Bobby sat in the other, and Toby leaned up against the file cabinet. The bags of food from Nancy's Diner sat on the desk, untouched. The hamburgers and fries would have to wait.

I took a sip of my coffee and stared out the window into the cold darkness. A couple hours ago I'd discovered my niece in the same barn I'd been held captive in. Sure, the trip back to the location of that strange and terrifying ordeal was a short one, but it had stirred up a mess of uncomfortable memories. Most of the Amish were good, God-fearing, law-abiding citizens. A few weren't. Even though I had a lot on my plate with the shooting at the high school, I couldn't shake the feeling that there was something very ominous going on in the Amish community.

I turned back to the men. "That little punk threatened my

niece, Todd." I pointed a finger at him. "There must be some way to get that search warrant."

"Oh, there are several ways, Serenity, and you know all of them. You want to do it the right way, I assume—in a way that you'll get a conviction that will keep the Swarey kid in prison for more than just a few months on drug charges."

"Drug charges that led to the death of a teenage girl," Toby chimed in. "Isn't he eighteen?"

Todd flipped through the file on his lap. "Yeah, but he was still seventeen at the time the incident with Taylor took place."

I leaned over my desk. "Jackson Merritt was there that night, too. It was his foster sister who died. The white residue you found in his flannel pocket, Bobby, was heroin. Maybe we could use that angle. The judge would sign anything I asked him to if it was connected to the shooting. The town's citizens want to strike out at someone, anyone, for what happened at the school."

Bobby straightened his glasses. "Monroe Swarey was on our peripheral during the serial killer case. He wasn't directly involved, but he came on our radar when we learned he was dealing drugs to the Amish kids." I nodded my head and motioned for him to continue. "It was at that time we discovered his mother was missing—and that she'd presumably run off."

Even on my best days I wasn't a patient woman. "Yeah, we know all that. What are you getting at?"

"Out of the blue, a couple months later, we have an inquiry about another missing woman—Charlene Noble." Bobby twirled the corner of his mustache.

Toby came over and spread his hands on the edge of the desk, beside Bobby. "Her sister from Indy contacted your office. She told me Charlene was a middle-aged wild child—the type of woman who was known to disappear for a while and then show back up again. But the sister thought two months was out of the ordinary for Charlene to not have contacted her at all. They have an elderly mother who has health problems. Even when Charlene was on one of her road trips, she checked in occasionally to see how her mother was doing."

"So Charlene Noble may or may not really be missing," Bobby concluded. He turned sympathetic eyes on me. "I know you've had a rough year of it, Serenity, and many of the crimes were committed in the Amish settlement, but in this case, you might be paranoid."

I tilted my head and exhaled slowly. Todd quickly averted his gaze, looking down at the file in his lap. Toby raised a brow at me, waiting to see how I reacted.

"Then what do you think happened to Erin Swarey and her friend, Charlene? Do you think it's just coincidence they're both missing?" I asked, trying not to sound offended.

"Absolutely not. I would wager wherever they are, they are together," Bobby replied.

Toby beat me to the punch. "You think they just ran off somewhere?"

"It's a reasonable assumption. The little girl told you she saw the two women together at the market. If Nicolas was an abusive husband, and all evidence warrants that assumption, then perhaps Charlene helped get her friend away from the situation. Maybe they're just laying low."

Bobby's words swirled in my head. "So you think I'm over reacting?"

"Not exactly. You and the Marshal should follow up on any leads that arise about the missing women, but"—he hesitated and softened his tone—"you have a more important investigation to worry about, here in town. The school shooting is national news. You should focus on that." I began to open my mouth and he raised his hands, interrupting me. "You mustn't always jump to sinister conclusions when a case involves the Amish people. Surely, after everything that's gone on in that community lately, they're due some peace and quiet."

Bobby was usually the voice of wisdom and reason. I always respected what the town's coroner had to say, and his expertise had helped solve many Blood Rock cases. But maybe he was being too optimistic, believing lightning couldn't strike so many times in one place. Yeah, a lot of crazy shit had gone down in the community, and they were due a break, but that didn't mean they were going to catch one.

Toby eyed me, and I got the feeling he already knew what I was thinking. Todd looked up nervously.

"I appreciate your frankness, Bobby. I really do. I am focused on the shooting case."

"I hear a *but* coming…" Bobby smiled slightly.

"My gut is shouting at me that there's more going on with the Swareys than just drugs and an abusive man. I pray I'm wrong, but I fear those women are in trouble. What kind of law officer would I be if I ignored my instincts?"

"Amen, sister," Toby pounded the desk, but I didn't look his way. I was studying Bobby's facial expressions. I wanted him to see why I was becoming obsessed with a case where we weren't even sure if a crime had been committed. I wanted his approval that I was doing the right thing.

"Are you sure it's not just revenge you're looking for? The Swarey kid threatened your niece and sold drugs to a girl that died. Since those two things happened while he was still a minor, you know it will probably only get him a short stint in prison. The father was abusive to his wife, but there's no evidence that he did anything nefarious to the woman." His gaze was unflinching. "If you were to discover that a more heinous crime had been committed, you could put the pair away for a hell of a long time."

I drank the last gulp of my coffee and opened the brown bag, pulling out a hamburger. For the first time in a few days I had an appetite. I had to keep my strength up and my mind sharp.

I looked around the room, making sure each man was listening carefully. "I'm good at multi-tasking. Keep the coffee coming and I'll get us through the school shooting case, and I'll continue to follow the leads about the missing women. With any luck, they're sipping margaritas on a beach down south somewhere. But if something ill-fated happened to them, I'm going to find out. As far as Monroe Swarey is concerned, I'm going to make sure he doesn't hurt anyone else again. He's going to pay for what he put Taylor through, too."

Silence settled in the office, like the snow falling outside.

"Are we in agreement?"

"I'll make those calls right away, boss," Todd said. He picked up his bag of food and left quickly.

Bobby was a little slower getting up. He turned to me and said, "I would have been disappointed if it was any other way, but mind what I said, Serenity. As long as it's not personal, it will stand up in court."

When I was alone with Toby, he took the seat Bobby had just vacated and dug into his bag. He popped a french fry into his mouth and grinned. "When it gets personal is when most of my cases are solved," he said.

I snorted. "My thoughts exactly."

23

TAYLOR

"You have company," Mom said, peeking inside the doorway.

"Who is it?" I tossed my tablet on the bed and slowly rose.

Mom's brows creased. "It's that Amish girl, Sarah. She said she wanted to talk to you." Mom spread her hands wide. "I hope you don't mind. I invited her in."

I pulled my long hair back into a pony tail and slipped on my tennis shoes. I tried to sound casual when I asked, "How did she get here?"

Mom crossed to the window and looked out. "There's a white van in the driveway. I can't see the driver, but it's still running."

I was almost through the door when Mom called out. "Taylor, be careful around that girl. The way she deceived you last night was wrong. You have enough on your mind to worry about. Don't let her drag you into her drama."

I stared back at Mom, realizing how different she was from

Aunt Reni. They were both blonde and slender. Aunt Reni was a little taller than Mom, and where Mom had lines around her eyes and mouth from smiling a lot, Aunt Reni's face was serious and smooth. Mom was optimistic and Aunt Reni usually expected the worst from people. My mother was cautious and lacked curiosity. Aunt Reni was always ready to jump head first into danger. I could see it in Mom's eyes—she didn't want me to talk Sarah. But if Aunt Reni was standing there, she'd probably want me to get information that might lead to Monroe's arrest, or maybe even find out where his mother was.

"I'll be okay. She's not that bad. I think she means well," I said quietly.

"Usually, I like to give people the benefit of the doubt, but after what happened with your brother and that poor girl, Naomi Beiler, I'm wary of those people. Your aunt has dealt with a lot of chaos in that community recently. I'm just not that open-minded about them."

I took a few steps and hugged her tightly. "You're my mom. You're supposed to worry about my friends. It's part of the whole raising a teenager thing. But Sarah's just a kid like me. I think she needs a friend."

I waited for Mom to nod and when she did, I was out the door and jogging down the staircase. I stepped into the kitchen and found Sarah standing next to the table, with fingers intertwined in front of her. Her white cap, maroon dress and black, laced up boots looked especially out of place in my house.

"Is everything all right?" I moved closer to her. "Were your parents really mad?"

"The bishop and ministers will decide my punishment next Sunday, and that will probably involve a couple of weeks of shunning. At least that's what Mama thinks." She frowned.

"She wasn't too upset, just disappointed that I hadn't talked to her about what was going on with Monroe."

"That's pretty much what my mom said too."

"Dad was another story. He hasn't even spoken to me since he took me home." She shrugged. "I guess silence is better than ranting."

The corner of her mouth quivered and I tilted my head. She giggled and I smiled back. Sarah had a lot of spirit, and at that moment I decided I really liked her.

When she quieted, I whispered, "Why are you here?"

She trailed her finger along the top of the kitchen chair and glanced around. "This is a beautiful house. No wonder Naomi wanted to run off with your brother."

"They were in love. If he had lived in a shack, she'd still have left with him," I said forcefully. My skin tingled as I stared back at Sarah, but my anger was quickly replaced with pity. I saw in her eyes how much she wanted to be English.

She put her hand on my shoulder. "I didn't mean to offend you. I was just imagining how Naomi must have felt being here with your brother. She could have worn denim jeans and cute tops." Her gaze drifted to the side as if she was looking at a picture of what she was describing. Her face came alive. "She would have been able to drive a car, and go wherever she wanted without a chaperone. No one would have judged her for the things she wanted to do. She might have even gone to college and become a professional working woman." Her eyes clouded. "If David Lapp hadn't killed her, that is."

It was difficult to breathe. I managed to push a breath out and slumped down in a chair. Sarah remained standing. She stared at nothing.

"Naomi was my friend. I sometimes have nightmares about what happened to her. It was incredibly unfair."

"Yes, it was," she mumbled.

"Do you wish you could leave your community, the way Naomi tried to do?" I said carefully.

Her frown returned. "Sometimes I want it more than anything in the world, although I don't know what I'd do without Mama and my little sisters and brothers. I couldn't leave them. I'd miss them all too much." She fretted with her hands. "I've seen firsthand what my family does to those who leave our people—just look at what happened to Daniel. He went something like fifteen years without a relationship with them. I can only imagine how tough it was for him."

Heavy sadness settled around Sarah and my mind couldn't help drifting back to the hallway and all those dead people. So many families would never see their kids again. It was hard to wrap my mind around a scenario where a family would eliminate their children just because they wanted to live a different lifestyle from them. Maybe if they saw what I saw in the school, they would act differently.

I wanted to help Sarah, but I didn't know what to do. Will had tried to save Naomi, and look what happened to her. Not that I thought Sarah would be murdered if she left the Amish, but I knew how hard it had been for Naomi to make the choice to leave. At the same time, it might be just as difficult to stay behind.

I grasped for something that might raise her spirits. "Aren't there any Amish boys you like?"

Her cheeks reddened and the corner of her mouth shot up. "Why, have you heard gossip?"

I snorted. "You're the only Amish person I talk to, Sarah.

My conversations with Matthew were pretty much limited to hi and bye."

She looked around again and then pulled the chair out beside me. She plopped down and scooted it closer. "There is someone I like, and I think he's sweet on me, too." She paused and her face was thoughtful. "At least he's been more attentive lately." I raised my brows and she went on. "He offered me and Christina a ride home in his buggy from the ball game the other night. He's never done that before, and he kept staring at me during church service last week."

I was relieved her mood had lightened and plowed on. "Well, who is it—is he cute?"

Her lips tightened and even with afternoon sunlight spilling though the windows, her eyes darkened. "Promise you won't be mad, Taylor."

The blood drained from my face and my heart sped up. I knew who she was going to say.

"It's Matthew," she said. "That's why I stopped by. Well, one of the reasons."

"What was the other?" I forced the words out.

"To apologize for last night. I'm sorry I lied to you. I feel terrible that we scared you—that we fought. I want to be your friend, and I should have trusted you with the truth."

I absorbed what she said, and thought back to how I felt about Lindsey sneaking around with Matthew. I never approved of the relationship, even though I was too afraid to say anything to my friend about it. I often wondered if Naomi hadn't been murdered, would love have been enough for her and Will? Daniel wasn't Amish anymore, but there were still issues between Aunt Reni and him that were because he used to be Amish. It was probably for the best that Matthew and Sarah got together. They had the same culture and understood each other in a way Lindsey and Matthew never could have. Still, a part of me wanted to defend my friend, who was still in the hospital, recovering from a gunshot wound. Lindsey would be so upset when she found out. I'd probably be the one who had to tell her.

I shook my head and met Sarah's anxious gaze. She was my friend, too. Maybe it had only been for a few days, but we'd experienced a lot together in that short period of time. She reminded me of Naomi, who I missed so much. That was enough for me.

I smiled a little. "It's okay with me. I think the two of you make a better couple anyway. It's for the best."

Sarah smiled back and she was radiant. "Oh, thank you. I was afraid to lose your friendship."

"It'll take more than being dragged to secret barn meetings and stealing my other friend's boyfriend to lose me, Sarah. I'm not going anywhere."

"Do you want to spend the day together? I really do want to go to the craft store"—she must have recognized the doubt on my face, because she quickly added—"for real this time. Maybe we could grab an early dinner in town."

"I'll have to ask my mother, but I think she'll probably say yes."

She jumped up. "I forgot all about my driver. I hired Martha, so we have a ride if you don't want to drive."

I chuckled. "It's okay. I like driving, and I have almost a full tank of gas."

Sarah hurried out the door to talk to her driver, and I slowly climbed the stairs to find Mom. I felt like I was betraying Lindsey.

Before I reached the top step, an idea blossomed in my head and my mood lifted. I just hoped Sarah would agree.

24

SERENITY

I scratched Hope's head, holding the phone away from my ear. The mayor had been rambling loudly for several minutes. I was about to interrupt him when he finally finished talking.

"Right. I met with the feds an hour ago and I'll be ready for the governor's visit tomorrow morning. I've got it under control." Before the man could start up again, I said goodbye and hung up.

Hope licked my fingers and I mumbled, "You're so lucky you're a dog, and not the sheriff. This is one of those days I'd like to trade places with you."

"I'm not sure I'd appreciate that." Daniel's voice rose up from behind me.

My heart froze, and then I relaxed. "Stop doing that," I growled.

"What?" Daniel replied in an innocent tone. Before I could remind him that I hated when he snuck up on me, he bent down and peppered my neck with kisses.

I leaned into him and let his mouth kiss away the bloody images from the crime scene photos of the school massacre I'd been pouring over that morning. I'd gone over the evidence with four federal agents and eight state officials for around six hours. The visit to the school was the hardest part. The bodies had been removed of course, but puddles of blood and other fluids spotted the hallway. Book bags still littered the floor. Within a day or two, the crime scene would be thoroughly cleaned and all personal belongings returned to the families. Whether any of the surviving Blood Rock students would be able to walk down that hallway again was another story. Psychological damage in cases like this was very real. The survivors were also victims, and it might be too much to expect any of those kids to feel safe or comfortable in that wing of the school again.

Daniel lifted his head and moved around in front of me. He dropped to his knees and looked up. Concern was etched on his face. "Are you all right? I can tell your mind is elsewhere."

I pressed my lips to his. For a glorious few seconds our mouths moved together, but then the horrifying pictures sprang up in my mind and I broke off the kiss.

"It's been a rough day. I was at the school for hours. There's talk of tearing down the section that the shootings took place in and rebuilding. The mayor already said he doesn't want to take funds away from the town's budget, but the state said they'd open a committee with local authorities to look into it."

He balanced on the balls of his feet, resting his hands on my knees. He had on a blue and red flannel shirt and tan work jacket. I loved the rugged look and the soft feel of the shirt's material when he hugged me. Even the bristles of his stubble against my cheek had an effect on me. He smelled like the snowy outdoors and I cursed my fluttering stomach. Mostly I was just surprised he was all mine.

"If I was a teenager attending Blood Rock High, I'd hate to have to be in that hallway every day, and I'm sure most parents wouldn't want their kids to be asked to be taught in a place where their friends and teachers were massacred." Hope pushed between us and Daniel rocked back on his heels, stroking her speckled chest. "Do you remember that sick bastard who shot those little girls in the Amish schoolhouse in West Nickel Mines?"

"Of course. Lancaster, Pennsylvania, about ten years ago." A shiver passed through me as I thought about how that particular killer had held the girls hostage for more than a half hour before he began shooting with a 12 gauge pump-action shotgun. Those girls knew they were going to die, and still they'd stood bravely in the face of depraved evil. "It happened so fast for the Blood Rock students that many of those kids were dead within a minute of the first shots being fired. The Amish girls' ordeal went on much longer."

He nodded. "The Nickel Mines community demolished the schoolhouse a week later. They rebuilt at another location. The new schoolhouse was designed differently from the one that the tragedy took place in. The community realized that in order for everyone to heal, there had to be no constant reminders of that fateful day that took the lives of five of their children."

"The mayor should learn a lesson from the Amish people. Sounds like a good idea to me, but with government bureaucracy involved in rebuilding, I'm afraid it will take Blood Rock a hell of a lot longer than a week to get the job done," I said.

Daniel's hands rested pleasantly on my thighs, but his face was gloomy.

"Have you talked to your sister today?"

"Briefly. Taylor fessed up and told her everything. I think Laura's in shock. It was only a year ago that she was dealing with Will and his tragic relationship with Naomi. And now Taylor is getting mixed up with the Amish."

"Usually it's the other way around—Amish parents worrying about their children's involvement with outsiders," Daniel countered.

"Hm. That's a pretty funny thing to say after everything I've personally witnessed in Blood Rock's community."

Daniel leaned back. "Kids are kids no matter the culture. I have to admit, things have turned especially menacing in the past couple of years."

His mouth was tight and his eyes were sad. I slid out of the chair and wrapped my arms around him, finding his mouth with mine. Even after a year of dating and then becoming engaged, our kisses still made my knees tremble. I loved the feeling of surrender. These were the rare moments when I could let my guard down and just relax—or try to.

Even for the rush of warmth in my belly, I still couldn't forget the crazy schedule ahead of me. My body must have given me away. Daniel let go with a heavy sigh.

"I know, I know, you have to leave," he muttered. His face was still close enough that his breath mingled with mine.

"Hopefully, I won't be too late." I stood up.

Daniel rose when I did. He cupped my chin. "What about the wedding, Serenity? Are we going ahead with it?"

My face flushed with heat and my stomach tied in knots. I had so many more important things on my mind than a wedding. I saw the desperation in Daniel's brown eyes and it softened my tongue.

"I just don't think this is a good time for it. Is it such a big deal to move the date a little?" I coaxed.

His frustration showed in every word he spat out. "There will always be a crime to solve or a person to save. You'll just keep moving the date back."

"No, I won't." My temper flared. "Twenty-three teenagers and three teachers were gunned down in Blood Rock's high school this week, Daniel. It's not right for the sheriff of the town to celebrate a wedding."

"It's officially off?" he pushed.

I pointed my finger at him. "You have no right to be mad at me. I'm not canceling the wedding, just delaying it until it's the right time."

"I'm not mad. It's exactly what I expected from you. It will simply never be the right time for you."

He strode past me and I called out, "Daniel, wait!"

But he didn't stop. When the door slammed behind him, I dropped to my knees and hugged Hope. At least the dog didn't have any expectations—besides a full bowl of dog food and a daily walk.

I loved Daniel, but I'd make a shitty wife. He wanted children. I'd be fine without any. He had a deep faith in God. In my line of work, I only saw the evil in the world. He was raised in a culture where women stayed home and cooked and cleaned. And I lived off fast food and dining out most days.

I was doing Daniel a favor if I didn't marry him. It would probably be the best thing for me in the long run too.

But why then was my heart breaking?

25

TAYLOR

Sarah blushed and then giggled when Nancy scolded her for not ordering the deluxe bacon burger.

"It'll put curves in all the right places, girl." When Nancy hovered over the table, her cleavage couldn't be ignored. "Trust me. Those Amish fellows like a little meat on their women."

Sarah brought a napkin to her mouth to stifle her small squeal of laughter. Nancy was old enough that she didn't have any shame left, at least that's what Aunt Reni always said. She also was a red head. It used to be natural—now she dyed her hair the flaming color. Everyone was used to her teasing, but it was a new experience for poor Sarah.

Sarah set her napkin down. Her face twitched when she said, "Well, you've talked me into it, Miss Nancy. If your famous bacon burger will endow me as well as it has you, I'm all in."

Nancy winked at me. "Good call. I'll add on the fries and have it out to you in a jiffy."

When Nancy was gone, Sarah exhaled. "She's a funny woman."

"Yeah, she likes to make people squirm. I hope when I'm old I'll be that entertaining."

Sarah giggled again and took a sip of her cola. She looked around at the busy diner. The drone of everyone talking and the clinking of silverware on dishes filled the air.

"There's so many people," she said with wide eyes.

"The diner always has a good crowd, but I think it's even busier than usual today," I commented. "Probably because of the shootings."

Sarah's smile disappeared. "Such a terrible thing." Her eyelids flickered. "How are you holding up?"

"As long as I'm not thinking about it, I'm okay," I admitted.

"When do you go back to school?"

The people sitting around the tables and in the booths blurred. "I don't know for sure. Mom said school officials are thinking about moving some classes into the middle school for the time being."

"It's going to be hard going back, isn't it?"

My head felt stuffy when I met Sarah's gaze. "Harder than you'll ever know."

"Is there anything I can do to help you?"

Guilt stabbed at my insides, but I plowed on. "Actually, there is something, but it's not really related to what happened at the school. It's something that would make me feel better, I think."

She crossed her arms on the table. "Anything. I'm here for you."

"I'm sure this will be kind of weird for you, but it would mean a lot to me if you came over to the hospital with me after we eat."

"The hospital?" Sarah's eyes widened even more.

"To meet Lindsey. She was shot, you know. She's doing a lot better, but I think it will help her to meet you in person."

She paled, but managed a determined look on her face. "Of course I'll go. She might not want to see me, though."

"We don't have tell her about Matthew today. It might help her deal with the breakup later if she gets to know you. Just a feeling I have." Sarah's lips puckered and I laughed. "It's going to be okay. She's a nice girl." I spotted Nancy squeezing between two tables and heading our way. "For now, let's focus on one thing only."

A glint of playfulness returned to her eyes. "What's that?"

"Putting some meat on our chests." I said it with the straightest face I could muster.

Sarah's head swiveled and when she spotted Nancy she began to laugh right along with me.

26

SERENITY

"**Y**ou seem distracted. Anything up?" Toby asked.

I glanced over at him. Between his cowboy hat, sunglasses, and mustache, you couldn't see much of his face. The sun glared off of the icy layer of snow that covered the fields as we drove past. My stomach always tightened when entering the settlement and this time was no different.

"I got into a fight with Daniel," I said. I would have felt more comfortable talking to Todd about it, but Toby was the one sitting in the seat beside me. He was a lot like me—a career lawman who seemed to have a difficult time having a personal life. The fact that he was helping me with this investigation when he could have been in a bar in a faraway city, sipping a strong drink, kind of proved my point.

"What did you do," he chided.

I grunted and smirked back. "Why do you assume it was me, and not something he did?"

He chuckled. "That man adores you. I find it hard to believe that he'd do anything to rile you up intentionally."

His words settled on my numb mind. He was right. Once again, it was my fault.

"We're supposed to tie the knot in a couple weeks. You know, like a Christmas wedding sort of thing." I eyed him, waiting for a shocked drop of his mouth, but was disappointed when he simply stared back, waiting for me to continue. "I don't think it's the best time to celebrate."

"Ah, I see." He paused, rubbing his chin. "And Daniel doesn't want to delay the big event?"

"Naw, it's worse than that. He thinks I'm purposely delaying it, and that I'll never actually walk down the aisle with him."

"Kind of like that movie with Julia Roberts?" He grinned.

"Something like that."

I slowed the car when we came up behind a black buggy. As we rounded the curve, the trotting horse came into view. Steam shot from the horse's mouth and off of his brown back. Toby leaned forward, abruptly more interested in watching the spectacle than in talking to me.

"Quite a sight," he mumbled.

Once I had broken lines and a clear view, I passed by the horse and buggy. Someone behind the small window waved and Toby returned the gesture.

"You live in a marvelous place, Serenity." He turned back to me. "Getting back to your cold feet—"

I interrupted him. "I don't have cold feet. I want to get married. I just can't concentrate on something that seems so trivial when I'm the sheriff of a town that just experienced the third worst mass school shooting in the country."

"You're not fooling me," he removed his sunglasses. "I get it. You don't have to be guilt ridden or anything. Not all of us are meant to settle down." He exhaled. "People like you and me have seen too many atrocities to convince ourselves that a blissful utopia exists. 'Cause it sure as hell doesn't."

"Wow. You sound pretty bitter." I slowed for another buggy.

"I'm happy enough with my life. I like going it on my own. There's no one to placate on a daily basis, and no one telling me what to do. I don't have to worry about leaving behind a wife and kids if I'm killed on duty."

The last part touched a nerve and I blew out a long breath. "I don't know if I even want kids, but Daniel definitely does. Most guys do, and he grew up Amish, so I think the urge to have a large family is even stronger for him."

"Have you talked to him about kids?"

I shrugged. "Kind of, I guess. What bugs me is that I've been honest with him, but I get the feeling he thinks I'll change my mind after we're married—that I'll suddenly want to pop out a few kids."

"I doubt that. He has to know what he's getting with you, and he's probably all right with it."

"I can't help but shake the feeling I'd be ruining his life if I married him. I'm not going to change that much, and neither is he. It might be a huge disaster."

"No one would ever marry if they thought as hard about it as you do."

"I don't know what to do." I thudded my head back against the headrest.

"Do you want some good advice?"

I nodded, not taking my eyes off the road.

"If you do get hitched, realize it's not going to be a stroll in the park—more like riding a bronco—and I'm sure there will be a lot of good mixed in with the bad. But if you walk away from the stoic Daniel Bachman, you give me a call. I promise I won't be a pain in the ass about the job. I'd rather not procreate, either."

My cheeks burned. I dared a glance Toby's way. He dipped his hat and offered me a lopsided smile.

I thanked the universe when the gas station came into view. I pulled in and parked without responding to what Toby had said. I could toss it up as a joke, but something in the way he'd looked at me a couple of times told me he was dead serious. The idea of hooking up with the US Marshal wouldn't have been so bad if I wasn't already in love with someone else. A shard of me wanted to give Toby some hope. Daniel and I had argued, but we weren't finished. At least, I couldn't wrap my mind around it being over. Surely, Daniel would give me one more chance. But there was the possibility that if I didn't marry him sooner rather than later, he would walk away. He knew exactly what he wanted, and I was a bumbling idiot when it came to my romantic life.

I parked and changed the subject. "Do you have the file?"

He opened the door and puffed out a short laugh. "Sure do."

"Good" was all I managed to mutter.

The station was empty when we walked in. The guy behind the counter had stringy dark hair and a tattoo of a quiver and arrows on his neck. For the rough look, his eyes were sharp when I stepped up. His name tag read, *Brian*.

Toby handed me the folder, and I pulled out the pictures of Erin Swarey and Charlene Noble. The only one we had of Erin was from an out-of-state driver's license from nearly two decades earlier, but it would have to do.

I placed the photos on the counter. "Have you seen either of these two ladies in here before?"

The man bent over the counter and studied the pictures. He pointed to Charlene's photo. "Definitely seen that one. It was a while back and only once, I think." He picked up the pictured of Erin and brought it closer to his face. "Now this one looks like one of the Amish ladies who occasionally comes in." He pointed at the photo. "Hard to tell, since I only seen her with her hair up in the cap, but they both have the same nose. She's a lot older now."

My gut appraisal of the attendant was spot on. I surveyed the station and was relieved that we were still alone. "Did you ever see these two women together?"

Brian scratched his head. "I'm not really sure, maybe. Danielle would have been the better person to talk to. She and the Amish woman were close." He puckered his lips and a shadow passed over his already dark eyes.

"Is she working today?" I asked. Adrenaline pumped through my veins. I already suspected what he was going to say next in answer to my question.

"She's dead. ODed a couple of months ago." His tone was casual.

I glanced at Toby. He'd removed his sunglasses when he'd entered the station and his bright blue eyes sparkled with shock.

"Danielle Brown worked here?" I asked.

He nodded. "She was saving up money so that she could skip town and get her own place. The girl was messed up. She'd been passed around foster homes since she was eight years old, and she confided in me that she'd been sexually abused in some of those homes. Poor girl just wanted to get out on her own, where no one could take advantage of her."

"Danielle and this woman"—I pointed to Erin's photo—"were friends?"

"The Amish woman was trying to help Danielle. I guess one day they started chatting, and before long Danielle was spilling her guts to the woman."

"How do you know she was attempting to help Danielle?" I pulled out my badge and showed it to Brian. His face didn't change expression. He wasn't surprised. He'd known I was the law when I'd stepped up to the counter. "This is important, Brian. What exactly did Danielle tell you about this Amish woman and how she was going to help her?"

"I was going to tell you the truth without you having to flash your badge." He rolled his eyes. "The Amish woman was planning to leave town, and she was going to take Danielle with her."

27

TAYLOR

The sound of the monitor's steady beeping drew my eyes to the machine. The overhead light was dim and Lindsey's eyes were closed. I'd spotted her parents and little brother in the cafeteria when we'd walked by, and I urged Sarah to lengthen her stride to get to the hospital room quicker. We passed the nurses' station and no one had stopped us from entering the room. I was relieved to find Lindsey alone.

"Maybe we shouldn't disturb her?" Sarah said. Like me, she was staring at the machine and tubes hooked up to Lindsey's arm.

"I talked to her on the phone this morning. She's expecting my visit." I reached out and touched Lindsey's arm. "Lindsey, I'm here," I whispered, holding my breath.

She stirred and then yawned. Her eyes flicked and opened. She brought her arm that didn't have tubes attached up to her face. Once the sleep was rubbed away, she greeted me.

"About time you showed up. Mom has been driving me crazy, pestering me constantly about how I feel, and calling the nurses in every time I wince."

"That's what mothers do. My mom would be way worse."

She reached out and I took her hand. "I have something really important to tell you," she said quietly.

I jerked my head at Sarah. Lindsey followed my gaze and her mouth opened. "I thought we were alone."

She squirmed on the bed, pushing up into a sitting position. A large bandage covered the side of her head where the bullet had grazed her skull. Her hair on that side had been shaved off. Lindsey had retained her sense of humor after being shot and joked that she'd finally have a hip hairdo. I knew she was just being brave for everyone else's sake. Losing half of her hair was bothering her, but at least she was alive.

"I'm sorry. I didn't see you there." Lindsey smiled at Sarah.

"This is Sarah. She's Daniel's niece," I told her.

Sarah moved closer. "No worries. I'm sorry to intrude at all. I was with Taylor and she wanted to stop by to see you. I hope you don't mind that I tagged along."

"Of course not." Her face brightened. "Do you know Matthew Troyer?"

The color drained from Sarah's face and I winced.

"Why, yes, I do." She paused and bit her lip. "He's a friend of mine."

"I'm so happy you came with Taylor." Lindsey stared at the Amish girl. "Did he ever say anything about me to you?"

I felt so sorry for Sarah. I never dreamed Lindsey would begin interrogating her.

Sarah nodded slowly. "Why yes, he did mention that you were his friend."

"Oh, we're more than friends," Lindsey said.

"Lindsey!" I chastised. "You shouldn't talk about it."

Lindsey shot me a warning look. "No, I have to get this

off my chest. Since Sarah is Matthew's friend, it's the perfect opportunity." She returned her attention to Sarah. "After being shot at and nearly dying, and so many of my friends losing their lives, I've reconsidered my life and what I really want to do."

"What are you talking about?" Sarah asked, her tone limp.

"I'm going to become a psychologist. I want to help people like Jackson and Danielle, so they don't have to resort to drugs and violence when things get bad in their lives." Lindsey paused and looked between me and Sarah. "I had told Matthew that I wanted to become Amish to be with him, but if I did that, I wouldn't be able to go to college, and that means I couldn't have a career helping people."

I rested my hand on Lindsey's shoulder and her smile grew. "You were right, Taylor. Even though you were polite and didn't come right out and say it. Matthew isn't the guy for me." She looked back at Sarah. "Will you tell him for me, Sarah? Since you're his friend, it might sound better coming from you. Who knows, maybe the two of you can get together someday," Lindsey joked.

A dozen emotions flicked across Sarah's face. When her smile joined Lindsey's, my heart finally calmed.

"I'll tell him, and don't worry. Matthew is resilient. He'll understand your choice. It's a great thing you're doing—taking the opportunity to change something so terrible into something positive." A tear slipped down Sarah's cheek and she quickly wiped it away.

"No tears allowed in my hospital room. That's an order," Lindsey said lightly. When she turned my way, I cringed inside at her sudden somber expression.

"I still have to talk to you." She frowned, glancing back at

Sarah. "I guess it won't hurt for you to hear, since it involves your community and all."

I leaned closer to Lindsey. "What's going on?"

"I never told you, but I talked to Danielle sometimes. She said Jackson was forcing himself on her, and that he was the one who got her hooked on the drugs."

Sarah spoke up. "Did he always get the drugs from Monroe Swarey?"

"Yes," Lindsey replied. "I'm not sure how they knew each other, but Jackson and Monroe hung out." She lowered her voice and Sarah and I both crowded in closer. "I think Jackson was mad at Danielle because she was talking about running away. It had something to do with Monroe's mom, although I'm not sure what she had to do with it, except that Danielle mentioned her a couple of times."

"Was Erin Swarey going to help Danielle run away?" Sarah asked. Her face was pinched tight.

"I think so. Then Monroe's mom went missing and Danielle over dosed on drugs. Don't you think that's kind of weird timing?" Linsey said.

My heart thumped and I caught my breath. "What exactly are you saying, Lindsey?"

"That he killed her, too."

"Who killed who?" With sickening dread, I realized what she meant, but I had to hear it out loud.

"Jackson killed Monroe's mom," Lindsey hissed the words out.

Lindsey's mom stepped into the room with a nurse at her side. "Sorry, girls. Lindsey has to have blood drawn. You can stop by again tomorrow, Taylor."

I backed away from Lindsey and grabbed Sarah's hand, taking her with me. "I'll see you later, Mrs. Meade."

When we were free of Lindsey's room, we hurried down the hall and caught the elevator. I felt nauseous when I finally met Sarah's startled gaze. "I have to tell my aunt everything Lindsey said."

Sarah shook her head. "We should tell Monroe. He's a horrible kid, I know, but if Jackson killed his Ma, he might know something about it. Maybe that's why he sold bad drugs to Danielle—to hurt Jackson."

The elevator doors popped open and I followed Sarah until we passed through the automatic doors, leaving the hospital.

Finally alone again, I grabbed her arm. "Are you crazy? He might have killed me that night, and we know he's a drug dealer. We shouldn't go anywhere near him. We have to tell my Aunt Reni. She'll know what to do."

Her face twisted as the cold air turned her cheeks red. "I'm sure this is difficult for you to understand—the only time you were around Monroe is that fateful night in the woods when he was acting so awful and Danielle died. But Matthew and I grew up with Monroe. He wasn't always a terrible kid. His father used to beat him and his mother was miserable being Amish. He had it pretty hard, and that's why he does the things he does." She pressed her lips together. "If we can talk to him first, maybe we can convince him to turn himself in, and then the sheriff will go easier on him. Haven't enough lives been ruined?" Sarah implored.

A bitter breath filled my lungs as the wind picked up, spraying loose snow around the parking lot. Clouds moved swiftly to cover the sun, and I shivered. Monroe's fiery eyes stared back at me. I never wanted to see him again, and I didn't really care what happened to him, but the desperate look on

Sarah's face made me pause. Was it possible to save Monroe? Lindsey now wanted to become a psychologist to help mentally ill people, like Jackson, before they went nuts and shot up a school. Could we possibly make a difference in the young Amish man's life?

"I don't think it's a good idea..."

"Please, Taylor—we'll get Matthew to go with us. We won't be alone. There will be three of us and only one of him. What could possibly happen?"

A dozen chilling images of our mutilated corpses in a cornfield, and a dusty old barn rose up in my mind. "He has a gun, Sarah."

A puff of cold air spread from her mouth when she laughed. "He wouldn't have hurt you. He was trying to be tough." She grasped the sides of my arms. "If Monroe won't agree to talk to the sheriff, then I promise you, we'll tell her all of it."

My insides shouted, *No, don't do it!* When I spoke I was surprised at what I said. "Okay, we'll give him the chance to come clean, but I think you're going to be disappointed. Monroe Swarey isn't a good guy in disguise. I don't think he's much better than Jackson Merritt, or even David Lapp."

"Thank you, Taylor. I know I'm going to prove you wrong," Sarah insisted.

It began to snow just as we reached my car. I lifted my face into the wind and let the flakes melt on my face. I really hoped Sarah was right and I wasn't about to make the biggest mistake of my life. What worried me the most was what Aunt Reni would do when she found out we went to Monroe Swarey's farm to confront him ourselves. Because if there was one thing I knew about my aunt—she would definitely find out eventually.

28

SERENITY

I stared at the procession of passing buggies through the car window. The pounding hoof beats reverberated in my head, pinching the slight headache that was developing. The sun was still high in the sky, and I glanced at my watch. There just wasn't enough time to drive out to the Swarey farm to talk to Nicolas and Monroe. I still had one more meeting to get through in town before I'd be free.

"Is it just coincidence that the girl who ODed in a park has a foster brother who becomes a mass murderer, and they both had connections to the Amish community and Monroe Swarey?" I turned to Toby, who was flipping through the pages of the file he'd created for Charlene Noble.

He glanced up. "Unlikely. But then again, I don't believe in coincidences." He held up a paper he'd jotted notes on. "The time frame Charlene's sister said Charlene went missing jives perfectly with Erin Swarey's disappearance. The girl, Danielle, ODed about a month after both women vanished. Less than two months later, Jackson goes on his shooting spree." He dropped the papers on his lap and tilted his head toward me. "Monroe Swarey, Erin's son, was the person who sold the drugs that killed Danielle. He threatened your niece, indicating he shares his father's violent tendencies." The corner of his mouth rose. "Do you really think that's all random happenstance?"

"No, but it's hard for me to believe that Monroe was involved in his mother's disappearance or even his father. We looked closely at both of them during the slain Amish girls' investigation." I hesitated. "I'm going to be sick if we missed something a few months ago."

"Do you want me to head out to the Swarey's farm while you're in town?"

I shook my head. "Don't take it personally, but you'll really freak them out. At least they know me."

The knock on the glass made me nearly spill my coffee. I rolled the window down and Bishop Esch leaned in.

"Sheriff, what brings you out to the community?" His bushy brows curved. "I hope nothing is amiss?"

The Amish leader was like a bloodhound when it came to police interest in any of his people. One thing I'd learned about the bishop was that he was a straight shooter.

I removed my sunglasses and eyed Aaron Esch. "We're following up on the drug overdose death of a teenage girl who worked here at the station." The Amish man's face remained passive and I took a gamble. "What would you say if I told you that it's come to my attention that Monroe Swarey was involved in the drug transaction?"

"Who gave you that information?" His voice was quiet.

"Let's just say it came from someone I trust." I stared back at him.

The bishop inhaled and blew out a rumbling breath. "I would say that the boy is touched by evil. If you have the evidence you need, you should put him behind bars."

I wasn't used to the bishop advising me to arrest one of his people. "You must really hate that kid," I said flatly.

He attempted to smile, but with his sharp, arctic fox-like features and coloring, it wasn't a gentle look. "I hate no one, even those that do me and my people harm. But I have lived enough years to be able to recognize and accept when someone's salvation is beyond my abilities. I have tried to work with the Swarey boy, teach him the right way, but he is stubborn and wild. His actions are affecting the other youth in my community. He is a poison that needs to be extracted. I fear that you, Sheriff, are the only person that can cure the illness growing here."

"That's getting right to the point," Toby said.

"I have lost patience. Nicolas can't control his son and neither can I. It's up to you, Sheriff, to take care of it." The bishop was steady and calm, like a mighty river.

The fact that he was encouraging me to arrest Monroe made me reluctant. The Amish always had their own agenda, and I suddenly had the prickling feeling that the bishop might know more than he was letting on. "What do you think happened to his mother?"

The expression on his face hardened, and I remembered his cold demeanor when he identified Naomi Beiler's body in the cornfield. "The woman was never truly one of us. She was an imposter. Who knows what kind of trouble she got herself into?"

I had to take a breath to compose myself. I also ignored Toby, who had gone from a relaxed slumping position to sitting up straight and still.

"That's rather harsh, Bishop. Erin Swarey was a member of your church for seventeen years. I'd hardly call her an imposter after that much time," I pointed out.

He snorted with a bellowing laugh. "She pretended until she couldn't lie to herself any longer. Don't get me wrong, I accepted her into our community with open arms when Nicolas brought her to us. But it's her influences that created what Monroe became."

"And his father, a violent and abusive man, had nothing to do with it?" I spat.

He backed away from the vehicle and lifted his shoulders slightly. "Nicolas has his own demons. I say if he hadn't been ensnared by that woman, he might have turned out differently." He fiddled with the end of his long beard. "It's funny how English women sometimes poison our young men. It wasn't long after Nicolas brought his bride to us that Daniel Bachman was spirited away by another English woman."

I gaped at the elder, chewing on my bottom lip and trying to gauge whether he was deliberately trying to goad me or just trying to make a point. He tilted his head idly, and I decided it was a combination of both.

"I don't have time for a philosophical discussion about the differences between Amish and non-Amish women, and the men who love them. Rest assured, I have my eye on Monroe Swarey. I just ask that you don't do anything to spook him. Let's keep this conversation between us."

"Of course, Sheriff. It's in my best interest to be discreet. I wouldn't waste any time if I were you. You never know what such a youth might do."

The bishop turned on his heel. His words replayed in my mind, *you never know what such a youth might do.* The cold breath I inhaled pricked my throat and goosebumps rose on my arms.

"Damn. Is he always so cryptic and creepy?" Toby asked.

"Unfortunately, yes. He normally likes to take care of policing his own territory." I met Toby's uneasy gaze. "The fact that he's so gung-ho, makes me want to tread carefully."

"Do you think it's possible that the Amish would cover for Nicolas if he did, in fact, do something to his wife?"

It was a good question, and one that had been rattling around inside my head since he stepped up to the car. "They have a vigilante streak, no doubt, but this particular leader tries to keep things as close to legit as he can. He is a good man at the core. Even if he didn't like Erin Swarey, I find it hard to believe that he would cover up for anyone hurting her. It's just not his style."

"Unless he felt she was dangerous to his people in some way. Look how he's trying to get rid of her son."

Toby's words sent a jolt through me. I couldn't ignore the truth of what he had just said. Maybe Aaron Esch was capable of finding a way to eliminate a woman, who he viewed as poison, from his community.

"Lord help him if he had anything to do with Erin's disappearance," I mumbled.

My phone rang and I picked it up. It was Todd.

"Hey, I'll be there in thirty minutes." I didn't bother with a greeting.

Todd wasn't interested in what time I was returning. I listened to him talk and closed my eyes. "Yep, got it. I'll make the call when I get there."

I hung up and turned to Toby. "Indy authorities found two female bodies in the White River. They're too decomposed to make a quick ID, but there are enough similarities to our missing women to get a hit in the database."

"How far away is that?" Toby asked.

I replaced my sunglasses and started the car. "Way out of my jurisdiction, and enough distance that it wouldn't make sense for a local person to dispose of the bodies there."

"Perhaps our mystery is solved."

It would be a sad outcome for the families, but they needed closure.

But then why was I still on edge?

29

TAYLOR

"Taylor!"

My fingers were on the car door handle when I heard my name being shouted. I turned to see Hunter jogging up to me. Sarah stopped on the other side of my car and waited.

"Hey, you haven't been answering my messages." He caught his breath.

My mind went blank as I looked at Hunter. "Huh?"

He pulled his phone from his pocket. "You know, text messages. I've been trying to get a hold of you."

I *had* been ignoring his texts. There was too much going on to talk to Hunter, but having him stand there in person had thrown me for a loop. Had he really just run across the parking lot to catch me?

I cleared my throat. "Uh, we're kind of busy right now."

He inhaled sharply. "I wanted to see how Lindsey was doing. I haven't heard anything new."

I couldn't help my brow from furrowing. "She's better. The

KAREN ANN HOPKINS

doctors think she'll be released from the hospital next week."
I turned to get into my car and he touched my shoulder.

"Wait."

I slowly faced him.

His voice softened. "How are you holding up? It was pretty intense what we went through at the school…"

Hunter's voice trailed off. A blond lock of his hair had drifted over the corner of his eye, and I had the urge to reach up and push it back. But of course, I didn't.

"It wasn't any more intense than having Monroe Swarey point a gun at me in the woods," I challenged. I felt a little bad when he leaned away from me. His nostrils flared.

"You know the guy's name?" he said incredulously.

For an instance I wondered what Hunter would have thought about the meeting with the Amish kids in the dark barn.

"Yeah, why does it matter?" I replied.

"Are you kidding me? He needs be in jail for what he did to you"—he paused, staring off into space—"and especially for what he did to Danielle."

"Don't worry, we're taking care of it." I had lost all patience. I wasn't looking forward to going with Sarah and Matthew to talk with Monroe, but I had promised her that I would. If Hunter stalled me any longer, I might lose my nerve.

Hunter looked over the car at Sarah and then back at me. "You and the Amish girl are…*taking care of*… the lunatic drug dealer *yourselves?*"

"Monroe is not a lunatic," Sarah said from the other side of the car. "He's having a difficult time and we're going to help him."

Hunter looked at me with pleading eyes. "That's not a good idea, Taylor."

My heart quivered and I watched a young couple walk

166

by, holding hands. Two small children skipped in front of them. The little girl squealed when her dad tossed a small handful of snow at her back. The child's laughter was music to my ears. The normalcy of the picture gave me some hope that Blood Rock wasn't in fact completely warped with evil.

I reluctantly returned my gaze to Hunter. "I promised Sarah I'd go with her and Matthew when they talked to him." My voice weakened. "I'm sure we'll be fine."

"You're going now?" His gaze drilled into me.

"Yeah." I opened the door and slid into the driver's seat.

"If you insist on being stupid, then I'm going too." Hunter quickly jumped into the backseat.

I swiveled around. "You can't come with us," I nearly shouted.

He leaned back and crossed his arms on his chest. "Why not?"

My mouth opened, but no words came out. I glanced at Sarah, who was already in the seat next to me.

She shrugged. "I don't care if he comes."

Hunter's face froze in a smug expression. He looked as if he'd grown roots into the backseat.

"What...about...your truck?" The words stumbled out of my mouth.

"I rode here with Josh and the guys. I'll simply text him to say I left with you." He began texting on his phone. "It'll get the gossip mill going, but it's the price I pay for being a Good Samaritan." He glanced up with a coy smile. "You can drop me off at my house later. I'm only a couple roads away from you."

"You know where I live?"

Sarah giggled, but abruptly stopped when I shot her the most menacing look I could manage.

"I just know things. It's no big deal." He didn't look up from his phone.

I started the car. I was annoyed that Hunter had taken it upon himself to be my bodyguard, but my heart also raced with the thrill of it. He wasn't such a jerk after all.

30

SERENITY

I rubbed my forehead as I left the conference room and walked down the hallway to my office. The gruesome pictures of the school's crime scene didn't get any easier to look at. Tomorrow's news conference would be the worst yet. We'd be officially releasing the stats on the kids and teachers killed. The contrast of their before the shooting and after photos were striking, and it left a hollow place in my stomach. Being able to connect the dots from Jackson Merritt to Monroe Swarey was becoming increasingly more frantic in my mind. Did Monroe's actions and Danielle's death set off the troubled teen? The little evidence we had pointed in that direction. Having a motive for Jackson going off the rails was not just important to me. Everybody needed some kind of explanation. Otherwise, the random horror of it all would make us a bunch of paranoid and helpless individuals. Knowledge was empowering in a case like this. The truth wouldn't bring any of the dead back, but it would at least make the citizens of Blood Rock feel that they had some control over their safety.

Daniel was waiting for me when I entered my office. He stood up and crossed the room, wrapping his arms around me. I sagged against him and pressed my face to his chest. Tears clouded my eyes and I couldn't speak.

"I'm sorry about the way I acted this morning. You take all the time you need, Serenity." He cupped my chin and tilted my head up. "I'll wait for you forever."

I sniffed and dabbed the corners of my eyes. The sun had set and snow was lightly falling. It looked cold and lonely beyond the window. Daniel's strong arms around me and his genuine smile were like a smack to my senses. This man was the main bright point in my life. With every new murder investigation, my mood had darkened. I was cynical and worried too much. Fun times were something most people took for granted. Not me. The beach honeymoon we were planning would be the first real vacation I'd taken in years. When I walked through the door, late at night, depressed about how hopeless society was, Daniel was always waiting for me. Just like right now, he wrapped his arms around me and chased the horrific images from my mind. If he wasn't in my life, I'd be lost.

I drew in a deep breath and looked into his eyes. "Are you okay with maybe just one kid in the sometime distant future?"

He looked surprised. "I didn't think you wanted children."

"I'm not sure if I do or not, but I love my niece and nephew, and they started out as babies. It might not be so bad." The tears threatened to fall again and I fought to hold them back. "Especially if it's something you really want. I don't think anyone regrets having a kid, but some probably feel remorse later in life if they didn't. I won't always put my job ahead of everything else."

"You don't have to say this for my sake. I want to be your

husband, with or without children." The side of his mouth lifted. "Making a baby would be something to look forward to, though."

I punched his arm and pulled out of his embrace. His teasing brought my emotions under control and I was good again. I certainly didn't want to break down in my office. I had too much to do.

"Is the wedding back on?"

His voice was so tentative I looked up from the other side of my desk and smiled. "I'm not guaranteeing we can pull it off with my schedule, but I'll try." I ignored the tingling feeling of panic spreading through me. "You weren't going to invite too many people, were you?" Before he answered, I rambled on, "Because it will be more likely to happen if it's an intimate gathering at the courthouse."

Daniel chuckled. "Didn't you look over the list I gave you a few weeks ago?" I shrugged and he shook his head in an, *I'm not surprised* way. "I'll take care of everything, Serenity. All you have to do is show up."

My nerves quieted. "All right. Sounds good to me."

"I was thinking about a different wedding venue," he said.

"What did you have in mind?" My stomach did a somersault.

His grin returned. "The old Arch building I'm renovating downtown is just about completed. There's a large room with hardwood floors and floor to ceiling windows. The tile fireplace is gorgeous and in working order. I talked to Mr. Arch and he says we're welcome to use it for our wedding."

I found it difficult to breathe. "That sounds kind of fancy for what we had in mind."

"All you have to do is walk through the door. I'll take care of everything else. I promise."

My mouth was dry and I felt queasy. Daniel was beaming, so I didn't say anything about how the thought of a formal wedding made me want to vomit.

The office door was ajar and the knock on it was quickly followed by the appearance of Toby and Todd.

"Wedding plans, eh?" Toby smirked at me.

My cheeks burned and I glared back at him for making me feel ashamed. I should never have talked to him about my reservations about getting married. "That's what people do when they're getting married." I avoided looking at Toby and focused on Todd's anxious face. "What's going on?"

Todd handed me the copy of a report and I scanned over it.

"One of the women found in the river was quickly identified using dental records, and she isn't either of our missing ladies," Todd said.

The morbid relief I experienced earlier was replaced with a racing heart. I looked up. "Then we need a search warrant for the Swarey farm."

"Will the judge grant it with only a little circumstantial evidence?" Todd asked.

I stood and placed my hands on the desk. "His grandson died of a heroin overdose last year. Given Monroe's connection to Danielle Brown and Jackson Merritt, I'm betting he'll be on board."

"You've had that in your back pocket this entire time?" Toby asked.

"I just wanted a little more before I pulled the card." I glanced at Daniel. "Aaron basically gave me permission to do what I needed to do to get Monroe Swarey out of his community for good."

"What if you don't find anything?" Daniel ran his hand through his hair.

"I already have enough to haul Monroe in for his connection to the drugs that killed Danielle Brown. As far as the missing women, I'm not so sure." My gaze flicked between the men. "Erin Swarey's and Charlene Noble's trails ended in the Amish community. That's where we have to begin."

"Do you want me to join you?" Concern was etched on the lines around Daniel's eyes.

"We're just going to take a look around and ask a few more questions." I forced a smile. "If the Arch building is going to be ready for our wedding, you need to concentrate on that project."

Daniel looked conflicted, but he finally nodded.

"Todd, I need you here to answer any calls that come in from the feds or the mayor. We'll"—I gestured at Toby—"head over to the courthouse for the warrant. Should be back in a few hours."

Several minutes later, I was getting into my patrol car when Toby said, "It's a mighty large farm to search in a few hours."

"It's enough time to take a closer look and pick up Monroe Swarey," I said.

"What are your thoughts on the missing women?"

My headache grew worse as I started the car. The horror of the school shooting had occupied most of my thoughts lately, but Erin Swarey's disappearance had bothered me for weeks leading up to it. The revelation that her friend, Charlene Noble, was also missing catapulted the investigation to a more sinister level.

"It's been a while. I'm afraid whatever happened to those women wasn't good."

31

TAYLOR

I stumbled and Hunter's hand shot out to catch my arm before I went down in the snow. After I had both feet squarely beneath me, I tugged free from him. Sarah and Matthew were a little way ahead of us and I could hear the soft mutterings between them. The sun had set a few minutes ago, and now a gloomy semidarkness had fallen. The snowflakes fluttering down were large and our feet sank into the snow as we traveled along the narrow trail through the woods. The Amish kids had insisted we park my car in the neighboring field and trek the rest of the way to the Swarey's farm. This back way to Monroe's was supposed to provide us with an opportunity to have a secret talk with him without his dad finding out. When I'd asked why it mattered to Mr. Swarey if we talked to his son, Sarah snickered at me, saying something about me being clueless.

Hunter and I glanced at each other. I could tell he was just as nervous about sneaking up on the Amish drug-dealing teenager as I was. He stayed close by, and we frequently bumped shoulders. His eyes rolled several times when they met mine.

"Hey, slow down," I whispered loudly to the leaders.

Sarah stopped and turned around. Matthew went a few more steps before he looked back.

Matthew's checks were red. Tufts of hair stuck out from under his black knit cap. "We have to get there before Nicolas finishes work at the welding shop and returns home."

"You're going to an awful lot of trouble to save a guy that doesn't deserve it," Hunter said.

"Everyone deserves saving," Sarah replied. "Maybe if your people were more forgiving, you wouldn't have a teenager shooting up your school."

Hunter's mouth dropped open and his eyes became slits. I placed my hand on his chest. "I talked to my aunt about it. She said some people have mental problems that they hide very well, and then one day they just explode." I leveled a stern look at Sarah and felt all of my own guilt slip away. "There wasn't anything we could have done to prevent Jackson from doing what he did. Just like you couldn't stop David Lapp from killing Naomi."

"Some people are just lost causes, Sarah." Matthew stepped up behind her. "You know that."

She swung around, her blue skirt swishing beneath her black jacket. "Do you think Monroe is a lost cause, too?"

Matthew's mouth twisted and he raised his head. Snowflakes swirled in between the trees and landed on his face. "I don't know about that, but he sure has problems. I'm not sure we can help him."

"You agreed to come, though. I thought Monroe was your friend." Sarah's voice rose.

"I came for you and Taylor. Monroe hasn't been my friend for a long time." Matthew dared to return his gaze to Sarah. "He's scary, Sarah. If you'd been there the night he threatened Taylor, you wouldn't want to talk to him at all. I realized then just how far gone he really was, and I've avoided him ever since."

Sarah sighed with a heavy breath. She turned to me. "I'm sorry I spoke so harshly about your school shooting. Of course it wasn't your fault, but it makes me wonder if Jackson had *real* friends, maybe he wouldn't have killed all those kids. We have an opportunity to help Monroe." She took a step closer to Matthew. Her voice was pleading. "He's still with us, and we might be able to help him. Shouldn't we at least try before it's too late for him, too?"

Hunter rubbed his forehead and Matthew stood quietly, his arms tightly folded across his chest.

I swallowed down the first reply that came to me. Sarah's eyes were desperate. She really wanted to save Monroe. She wasn't playing a game.

"We'll do what we can, but you have to prepare yourself that it might not work out the way you're hoping it will. Regardless of whether Monroe has friends, the law is going to catch up with him. He sold drugs to a girl that died from them," I said.

"It was an accident. I'm sure of it." Sarah's face became bright with hope.

Hunter snorted. "It won't matter. Danielle died. She was a nice girl."

"I'm very sorry for her. I know you're upset that you lost a friend, but Monroe isn't a bad person. He's just lost," Sarah insisted.

"We better get moving. The snow will light our way, but I'd rather get this over with." Matthew trudged away.

"Dude, I agree with you," Hunter chimed in.

I took Sarah's hand and we followed Matthew through the trees. Hunter was close behind us, and I was glad he was there. His presence made me feel like the crazy walk through the woods with the Amish teens wasn't a dream I'd wake up from soon. It was all too real.

Matthew raised his hand and hissed, "Shhh."

We stepped up behind him and I peeked around his shoulder. Snow covered hills were nestled between thin tree lines. Smoke puffed from the chimney of the white farmhouse, and there was a cluster of sheep next to one of the barns. They were eating from a round bale of hay and making soft bleating noises.

"Is that it?" I whispered into the cold air. Matthew nodded and we began moving again.

Everything looked harmless enough, but my skin prickled. With each step I took, my heart pounded harder. Suddenly, the chill pierced my coat, and I felt numb. I remembered what Serenity had said about listening to my gut.

But it was too late to turn back now.

32

SERENITY

I was still plodding through the snow to the porch when Toby knocked on the door. He peered through the window and looked over his shoulder.

"No one appears to be home," he said.

I looked at the area around the porch and then up at the chimney. "There's a fire going in the woodstove and there's tracks leading up to the house and back to the barns," I pointed out.

Toby joined me at the bottom of the steps. "It's hard to say how fresh they are. It's been snowing on and off all day long."

"True." The wind picked up and I shivered. The temperature was dropping and the snow on the ground was developing a crisp, shiny sheen on it. Darkness was complete, and the half moon was coming and going through the thickening clouds. I zipped up my jacket. "We'll start on the sheds and work our way back to the barns. Hopefully Nicolas or Monroe will arrive soon, and we can get into the house. I'd rather not force our way in unless we have no choice."

Toby nodded and followed me to the shed beside the house. We hadn't ventured into this one the last time we were here, so I wasn't sure what to expect when I pushed the door open. I flashed my light into the cramped space. Bumping into a push mower, I had to duck my head to avoid hitting it on a chain saw that was hanging from the low rafter.

Cans of oil lined the wall, and three bicycles were parked along the back of the small space. One was a woman's bike and the other two were for men. I imagined the Swarey family biking down a country road together. Thick dust covered them now.

Toby's voice broke the silence. "I checked land records. This farm is two hundred and forty-six acres. That's a lot of places to hide a body or two."

I grunted. He was right. I was still having a difficult time wrapping my mind around the possibility that while I was tracking down the Amish driver, Caleb, for the serial murders of three young women, Nicolas Swarey, who was also a suspect in that investigation, was murdering his wife and her friend.

"It's hard to believe that around the same time those poor Amish girls were being raped, killed and mutilated, there was another demented man just up the road carrying out his own demented acts on two more women," I mused.

"It would be sensational, wouldn't it?" He pushed his cowboy hat back and slanted to look at me in between the hanging tools. "I've found in many cases, where there's evil, it tends to run deep."

"You're more screwed up than I am," I commented, wrinkling my nose at the musky odor in the shed. Nothing seemed to be out of the ordinary, so I squeezed past Toby and walked out into the falling snow.

"That's why we get along so well." He shut the door behind

us and grinned like a wolf. "Sounds like you worked out your problems with your fiancé."

His tone was sarcastic and I rounded on him. He drew back when I jabbed my finger into his chest. "Look, I love Daniel. We have some things to work on, but I'm not going to be depressing and cynical for the rest of my life. I'm going to take a chance. I might regret it one day, but I'd rather have that kind of remorse than the kind you have when you're too chicken shit to take a risk. Yes, I'm going to trust another human being and attempt to be happy. Maybe you should try it."

The grin was cemented on his face. "That's exactly what I'm doing right here."

"Don't say something stupid like that." I started walking, not bothering to look back. I could hear his boots crunching in the snow behind me.

"You'll regret it, Serenity. Marriage and kids will be a disappointment to a woman like you."

"You're wrong. Daniel loves me and that's all I need."

"Do you love him?"

"Of course," I snarled.

A sound whistled on the wind and I stopped in my tracks. Toby nearly bumped into me. "What was that?"

A piece of metal from the nearest barn roof flapped in the wind and branches cracked against each other. A sheep bleated.

"What?" Toby's breath was warm against my ear.

"I don't know," I muttered. "I thought I heard a voice—like a wail."

"It's probably just the wind."

"Probably," I agreed, but I headed toward the barn with purposeful strides all the same.

33

TAYLOR

The hill was steep, and I lost my footing and slid down in the snow until my feet finally struck flat ground. Hunter helped me straighten up, and he didn't immediately release my arm when I had my balance. His helpfulness was confusing. Until the day of the shooting, he'd hardly shown me the time of day.

Matthew motioned for us to move faster and we jogged over. We caught up just as Matthew and Sarah disappeared through a small barn door. The wind felt like it was cutting into my face as I lifted it to the sky. Dark rimmed clouds were threatening, and only a thin shard of moonlight light shined. I took a deep breath and ducked into the shadows.

My senses were immediately assaulted with warm, moist air and a stink that made me cover my nose. Then came loud squeals and grunts from all around us.

I squinted into the darkness. "Are those pigs?"

"Afraid so," Hunter said. His hand reached back and brushed mine. I didn't hesitate and grabbed onto it.

Matthew said something, but I couldn't hear him with the angry pig noises sharp in my ears. We must have disturbed them when we entered the barn.

Sarah came back and said, "We have to get to the other side of the corral." She pointed across an expanse that came into view as my eyes became accustomed to the darkness. "We'll climb along the fence panels. Be careful!"

She swirled away before I could tell her she was crazy. Giant shapes, the size of ponies, moved in the pen. They bumped into each other and I saw flashes of tusks in the crowd.

I was sweating inside my coat and my pulse raced when I leaned closer to Hunter. "I don't think I can do it..."

"You don't have to. We can go back. These are ridiculous the lengths we're going to for a drug dealer who got Danielle killed." Hunter's eyes sparked.

Matthew and Sarah were already halfway across the pen. They had easily climbed the railing and shimmied their way past the annoyed swine. My heart throbbed into my throat as I watched the giant animals follow along below them. I could barely breathe from the rank smell and my stomach rolled with nausea, but my pride urged me to get over my fear and step up on to the metal pipe. I couldn't let Sarah down because I was terrified of pigs.

Ignoring Hunter, I grasped the higher rail and pulled myself up. The metal was slick with moisture and my hand slipped with my first attempt. I wiped my hand on my pant leg and tried again. This time I was able to hold onto the cylinder railing. Hunter quickly followed suit, but he was scowling. He didn't say a word and I was glad. I didn't think I could have spoken if my life depended on it. I was so focused on inching my way slowly across the livestock panels I couldn't even glance his way.

"You're doing great, Taylor," Sarah shouted out above the squeals.

A pig's snout brushed the bottom of my foot and I froze.

"Don't look down," Hunter ordered.

But my eyes had already strayed in that direction. A black and white spotted boar that must have been at least seven hundred pounds, looked back at me with a gaping mouth. Another pig rammed into it and they began snapping at each other. I stretched my legs and arms, scooting along the poles faster. I could see Sarah's face pressing against the railing on the other side. Her eyes were wide.

Sarah and Matthew had taken the pigs by surprise. By the time Hunter and I made the trip across the panels, they were worked up into a frenzy.

My hands slid along the wet pole and my foot slipped once, but I quickly drew it up. When I looked ahead, there was only a few more feet to go.

"Just take your time, Taylor. Calm down. We're almost there." Hunter's voice was steady and my heart slowed with the sound of it.

My foot came down and missed the railing. It swung for only a blink of an eye, but it was enough time for the black and white boar to hook it with its jabbing tusk. With a jerk, my leg was dragged into the pen.

"Hold on!" Hunter shouted. His hand swiped the air at me, but too late. Something pounded my leg, twisting my body and snapping my hands away from the wet railing. I fell backwards, landing on the back of the giant boar. It screeched and surged forward, knocking into a solid black pig. I clawed the darkness, but it was like being caught in a riptide. I had no control over my body. I bounced off of the boar's back and slammed into another one. Spots peppered my vision. Sarah screamed and then I was surrounded by legs and hooves as I sunk into thick mud. I didn't dare open my mouth. A hoof struck my cheek and then something landed on my stomach. I sunk deeper into the muck, until my arms were stuck in the stuff. Pain shot through my arm and I saw a pig's mouth around it.

Squeals, grunts, and shrieks flooded my ears. A hard jab tore into my leg, and then I was being dragged. The skin on my arm ripped apart. I couldn't see as everything blurred. The sounds of shouting and squealing grew fainter. A huge black object hovered over me.

My hand closed around something, and then the light disappeared altogether.

"Taylor, Taylor—open your eyes," a voice demanded.

I blinked until I could see again. Hunter and Sarah were kneeling over each side of me, and Matthew loomed over all of us with a glowing lantern. I tasted mud in my mouth and choked. Hunter pulled me up into a sitting position and my stomach rolled. I leaned over and spit up a gob of the putrid stuff. I kept spitting until my mouth cleared. Caked with black muck, warm wetness pulsed on my arm. I looked down and saw dark blood pooling on the bite wound.

Sarah yanked her scarf from her neck and wrapped my arm snugly. "Oh, my Lord. I thought you were a goner. You just disappeared into the pigs."

Memories rushed back and I gasped. "How did I...get out...of there?" I coughed out.

"Hunter jumped in. He kicked and punched the swine away from you, like he was a super hero or something." Sarah bobbed her head. "Matthew went into the pen, too."

The boys' legs were splashed with the same black mud that was all over me.

Tears welled in my eyes. The water works weren't because of the pain in my throbbing arm or shooting up my leg. Hunter squeezed my hand and Matthew offered a faint smile. "Thank you—both of you—for getting me out of there."

"They would never have saved you if it weren't for him. He's the one who climbed over the panels with a pitch fork and began swinging, so the boys could pull you out," Sarah said.

I followed her gaze. Monroe Swarey leaned against the wall. He was smoking a cigarette and his eyebrows arched wickedly when he saw me looking at him. His legs were splattered with mud. The fork Sarah had talked about was resting against the boards beside him.

I dipped my head in a curt nod and he smirked back at me.

"We have to get her to a hospital. She's lost a lot of blood," Hunter said.

"Her leg is bleeding too," Matthew commented.

I felt a jab against my thigh and I shifted my weight. There was a muddy object there—like a jagged rock. I reached for it and began rubbing the dirt away. My fingers found something long and slender. I pulled on it until it was free of gook. It was a shoe string.

I began wiping the thing even more vigorously.

"What's that?" Hunter asked.

"It looks like a tennis shoe," Sarah breathed.

Yes, I think Sarah is right, I thought as I turned it over and reached inside to scoop more mud out. My fingers touched something that made me snatch my hand back. Sarah's anxious face urged me on. I slowly pushed my fingers back inside and wiggled the object until it was free. Then I pulled.

Sarah was the first to cry out, but my scream wasn't far behind hers.

I tossed it on the ground and scurried backwards, bumping into Hunter, who nearly fell over.

Matthew brought the lantern in for a closer look. After a long pause, we all leaned over and stared.

It was part of a human foot.

My head snapped up and I looked for Monroe. He was gone.

34

SERENITY

The gust of blowing snow carried another sound that made the hair shoot up on my neck. I pulled my 9mm from its holster and began running in the direction of the pig barn. The snow pelted my face as I forced my legs faster.

"That was a scream, I'm sure of it," I shouted to Toby, who was running abreast with me. He had drawn his revolver.

"It's probably the hogs. They make noises like that." He took a gulp of air. "You heard them the other day."

I really hoped I was wrong and ended up feeling foolish, but I highly doubted it this time.

Toby reached the barn door first. He backed up to the side of it and waited for me to push it open. My hand grasped the handle.

"Drop your guns!"

Toby and I whirled together. Nicolas Swarey stood about twenty feet away. He aimed a shotgun at us.

I raised my gun and focused on his head. "Put your weapon

down, Nicolas. There's two of us and only one of you. You might get a shot off—but only one. You'll be a dead man."

He held the shotgun steady. "You have no business here, Sheriff. We've answered your questions and you already snooped all over the farm. Your behavior is turning into harassment."

His words startled me. Nicolas Swarey hadn't struck me as an overly bright man, or one with the ability to manipulate others. My first impression of him was that he was a religious zealot. He had been on my short list of potential suspects for the Amish girl killings because of his callous comments about how the girls had somehow brought on their torturous deaths themselves. I had also discovered he had had a violent past and had mutilated a couple of dogs who'd attacked his sheep the year before. But Nicolas hadn't been the killer in that case, and he'd slipped back under the radar once the investigation wrapped up. If it wasn't for his still missing wife and her friend disappearing after a visit to Blood Rock, I wouldn't have given the man much thought. His simmering anger had always been palpable, and his aloof and unfriendly attitude made people avoid him, but none of those things alerted me to the possibility that he was a real threat to myself or anyone else.

Now, staring down the barrel of his gun, I felt like a complete fool. How could I not see this coming?

"I have a search warrant, signed by the judge, to take another look around your house and farm. The warrant was granted because of a second woman's disappearance. Her name is Charlene Noble, and she's a friend of your wife's. We have eye witnesses that place Charlene in the community around the same time that your wife went missing. It makes perfect sense that we do a further search of your property. That's why we're here. Now if you'll just drop your weapon, we'll get on with our job, and you can avoid getting into any more trouble or being shot dead."

A sick smile lifted on his lips. It was snowing harder and flakes peppered his black beard. I ignored the sting from the icy wind striking my face and held my hands firm. My breathing calmed and the pounding of my heart slowed.

"If you don't put down weapon, I will shoot you." I shouted to be heard over the howl of the wind.

From the corner of my eye I saw Toby's gun drawn and aimed at Nicolas. His hands were as steady as mine.

"Do you really want to die today, Nicolas?" I asked.

"God is with me. He will guide my hand."

I saw the glint in his dark eyes and the twitch of his jaw. I squeezed the trigger.

The bullet shot into the sky when I lifted my gun at the last second. Nicolas was lying in the snow. Daniel stood over him with a two-by-four length of board.

"Nice job, Daniel," Toby said. He sprinted over to Nicolas and dropped down beside him, checking his pulse. "He's unconscious."

I replaced my gun in its holster and closed the gap. I grinned at my fiancé. "You have an uncanny gift of showing up at just the right time."

Daniel smiled back. "My sister called me. She's been having problems with Sarah. She wanted to talk to me about it."

"You were just driving by?" I held in a snort and shook my head in wonder.

"Pretty much. I saw your car up here and decided to see if you needed my help. Obviously, you did." He looked so pleased with himself, I laughed.

A whistling sound drew our attention to the nearest barn.

Daniel stepped around Nicolas and joined me. "Did Nicolas kill his wife?"

"After that little show, I'm beginning to think it's a real possibility."

"Let's cuff him and put him in the car. I'm going to call in back up," I said.

A shot rang out and I ducked. Daniel grabbed my arm and we ran to the stack of round hay bales for cover. Toby sprinted to the side of a shed. He poked around the building and fired in the direction of the incoming shots.

"Shit!" I exclaimed. I had my gun back in my hands and peeked around the edge of the hay.

"Do you think it's Monroe?" Daniel's voice shook with adrenaline.

"That's who I'm guessing. Dammit, it was supposed to be a simple search warrant. I didn't expect a gun fight."

"He's a troubled kid, Serenity." Daniel hesitated.

"And he's trying to kill us." I thrust my chin towards the place where Nicolas had been on the ground. He was gone.

"I don't suppose you have a gun on you?" I glanced at Daniel.

"I was visiting my sister—no, I didn't go armed." He pulled out his cellphone and cussed. "Damn, no reception.

"Now we're more evenly matched, and they have an advantage to knowing the farm a hell of a lot better than we do," I hissed, handing him my car keys. "You have to get back to the car and call this in. You'll probably have a bar or two at the house." He stared back at me with wide, unblinking eyes. "Go! I'll cover you."

"Dammit," he licked his lips and bent down to kiss me. "Be careful—please."

He took off and I left the cover of the hay, firing at the barn.

Toby saw what was going on and he joined me, giving me the chance to race over to him.

I drew in an icy breath that scraped the back of my throat. We both crouched, our backs to the shed.

"I must be losing my sense of intuition. An ambush was the farthest thing from my mind," Toby said with a grunt. He reloaded his revolver while he talked. "This is your jurisdiction. What's the plan?"

The Marshal was taking it in stride, and I appreciated that he was ready and willing to take orders from me. I eyed him. "Did you see which way Nicolas went?"

He shook his head. "We can hold our ground until back up arrives."

The sound of a shotgun blast broke the silence. It came from the direction Daniel had gone. My heart dropped into my stomach.

"Cover me—I'm going to him." I spoke with the urgency of a woman who might lose her lover.

A scream pierced the air and I stopped. My eyes met Toby's. It was a female voice, and it came from the barn.

"I'll go after Daniel. You help the woman," Toby ducked behind a tree and disappeared.

I forced Daniel to the back of my mind and raised my gun.

There wasn't any time to contemplate what the hell was going on.

I hadn't arrived early enough to save everyone at the school, but I had the chance to save whoever had screamed.

I left the protection of the shed and pounded my legs to cover the short distance to the barn. Snow swirled in between the buildings, diminishing my sight.

More gunshots pierced the night air.

35

TAYLOR

"Where did Monroe go?" I leaned into Hunter and he pulled me up into a standing position. "I don't know," Sarah said, looking around. "Better question is, who was that?" She pointed at the foot remains.

"I bet your friend Monroe knows exactly who it was." Hunter's voice was raw. "That's why you don't mess around with drug dealers—you end up getting fed to the pigs."

"We don't know what happened to whoever that was," Sarah argued.

Matthew put his hand on her shoulder. "Yeah, and we hardly know Monroe anymore. Let's just get out of here and tell the sheriff."

"Best thing I've heard all day," Hunter said. He turned to me. "Can you walk if I help you?"

I gingerly put some weight on the leg that was bitten and took a step. Even if the leg had been falling off, I would have said yes. I wanted to get away from that horrible place as quickly as possible. "I'm fine," I lied, gritting my teeth. "We can't leave it here—no one will believe us." I nodded at the foot.

Matthew jogged over to a room and pushed the door open. When he emerged, he had an empty feed bag in his hands. He grabbed the pitch fork from the wall and gave the bag to Hunter to hold open. He scooped up what was left of the foot and the muddy shoe, depositing them into the bag.

"Problem solved," Hunter said. "Now, let's get the hell out of this barn of horrors."

He grabbed my hand.

"This way," Matthew instructed. He slid in between a Bobcat and the wall.

The inside of the barn was like a giant maze. We passed closed stall doors, farm equipment, and a pile of manure that made me hold my breath. My arm throbbed and pain pulsed up my injured leg, but I didn't dare complain as Hunter tugged me through cobwebs. He bumped into a wall and exclaimed, "Why don't you turn the lantern back on?"

Matthew didn't stop. He glanced over his shoulder, "I don't think it's a good idea to draw attention to ourselves. You're carrying a foot and we have no idea where Monroe went."

The Amish boy's statement sent a shiver up my spine. He was right. We were in real danger.

Boom, boom.

I would never forget that dreadful sound. "What was that?" I stammered.

"Gunshots." Hunter tugged me faster.

We finally reached the end of the building. Matthew pulled on the door, but it wouldn't budge. He grunted as he tried harder.

"Who's shooting?" I asked no one in particular.

Tears ran down Sarah's face and she pressed in closer to me.

Hunter ignored my question. "I'm going to help him. We have to get out of here."

"The pain must be awful," Sarah muttered through wet lips. "You're really brave."

I lifted my shoulders. I wasn't brave. Fear is what kept me on my feet. The adrenaline rush is what allowed me to keep moving.

She stared at the scarf she'd tied around my arm. It was soaked with blood. She chewed her lower lip as she raised her gaze. "Hurry up, guys," she urged.

Several gunshot blasts boomed. Sarah trembled against me. The boys stopped prying on the door. There was silence, until the night was shaken by more gunshots popping beyond the barn walls.

Sarah mumbled something in her language. It sounded like she was praying. I closed my eyes. My head rolled with dizziness. I should have listened to my gut and not let Sarah talk me into coming out here to see Monroe. It was a huge mistake, and now we were all probably going to die. I wondered what the news would read—*teens survive school shooting to be murdered less than a week later at an Amish farm.* And my parents would have to bury their daughter. Would my death bring them back together, or ensure that they ended up getting a divorce? Tears welled up in my eyes. I couldn't stop the giggle that bubbled from my lips. My head was thick and dazed. It was just like that night in the woods—how stupid I was.

Sarah took a step back. "Stop it, Taylor!" she whispered. "You're scaring me."

I heard a tiny *meow*, followed by another *meow*. The noise came from a nearby stack of hay bales. I left Sarah and limped over to the sound, dragging my leg. A furry orange object streaked across the hay.

"It's a kitten," I murmured.

"Don't!" Sarah said. "You're acting crazy."

"We can't leave it here—"

Then I was tumbling through the air. My back struck the floor and pieces of hay sprinkled down on my face. A cloud of dust puffed out around me. I tried to cough, but a breath wouldn't come.

"Taylor, can you hear me?" Sarah called out from above.

I stared upwards while Sarah looked down. Hunter and Matthew were, too. The lantern was a round glow in the darkness above. They must have been twelve feet away.

"It's some kind of trap door," I heard Matthew say.

"Are you all right, Taylor? Talk to me!" Hunter demanded.

I gulped and air finally filled my lungs in a wheezing noise. I pushed up with my good arm. "I'm okay, I think." The words rasped between my cracked lips.

A scrapping noise snapped my head sideways. I was in some sort of small room. The light from above only illuminated a slight area around me. The edges of the room were in shadows. A terrible smell assailed my nostrils and I gagged. Several buckets were strewn around the dirt floor and there was a stained mattress in the corner.

Something scuttled in the shadows and my heart banged in my ribcage.

I wasn't alone.

"Did you come for me...?" The voice was week and hollow.

I screamed.

36

SERENITY

I slammed into the side of the barn and scanned my body for blood. The shots fired had come close and from the direction of one of the barn windows of the connecting hog barn. I swallowed a gulp of air and exhaled. The shooter was inside the same barn where I had heard the scream originating. There wasn't time to wait for back up or think up a grand plan.

I pushed the door open and slid into the dusty darkness. I blinked several times, and as my eyes became accustomed to the dimness, I moved forward slowly with my back against the wall. As long as I could see a little, I was leery to turn on my flashlight. Nicolas would know the interior of his barns better than me, but his sight was as limited as mine was in the semidarkness. I might actually be able to sneak up on him or Monroe without a light. I had already decided that Monroe must have been the person who shot at us when Nicolas was on the ground. Nicolas Swarey was a loner. Anyone in the community who might have called the man friend, wouldn't have shot at the sheriff. Monroe was protecting his father—that's the only answer that made any sense.

I bumped into a wooden table and sharp pain spread out from my hip bone. I bit my lower lip and walked faster, my eyes darting around the large room. I calculated where I thought the gunman was and went in that direction. Wind rattled loose boards and I strained to hear any other movement. There was a doorway ahead and I aimed for it. Thoughts of Daniel attempted to invade my mind, but I held them at bay. Toby would take care of him. I had to help the woman who had screamed. Visions of the mutilated corpses of Makayla Bowman and Hannah Kuhns kept me going. I wasn't there to help those girls, but I might be able to save a woman today.

I pushed the door ajar and peeked out, holding up my 9mm and ready to return fire. There was an empty alley between the two barns. Snow floated from the gaps in the wood and small drifts dotted the ground. I sprinted across the narrow space to the door on the other side.

My pulse quickened as I carefully went through the next doorway, but I welcomed the adrenaline rush. This cat and mouse game we were playing suited me just fine. I had a gun and I knew how to use it. I was the hunter, I told myself, not the other way around.

The pungent smell of the pigs flooded my nostrils and I began taking shallow breaths. I remembered the crowded pen where the animals were kept. I ignored their angry grunts and jogged along the wall until I came to two small windows. Moonlight sprayed in through the openings. There were several shell casings on the ground below them. I pulled up and looked around. The hogs were like giant shadows moving within the enclosure. I swallowed hard and strained to listen past the squeals. Nothing. There was another doorway further ahead and I jogged along the wall until I reached it. I pushed the sliding door sideways just enough to glimpse outside. Snow dropped heavily on the steep hill beyond the barn, and it was disturbed outside the doorway. I followed the tracks up the embankment and into the tree line.

I barely breathed. There were multiple tracks. Because of the depth of the snow, I couldn't tell if the lines were coming or going, but it appeared that at least three other people had been here.

"What the hell?" I mumbled and slipped back into the barn.

My eyes adjusted to the dim interior again and after taking a look around to see if the coast was clear, I followed the length of the pen. I stopped when I reached the end of the livestock panels and stared at the beasts. I had to get to the other side of the room, but the only way over seemed to be through the pen. There was no way in hell I was doing that. Time was ticking by and the lack of any more screams worried me greatly.

I jogged back to the doorway and went outside. My boots sunk down in the snow, but I worked them into a run and stayed closed to the barn wall. I was out of breath when I turned the corner and saw what I was looking for—another doorway.

I approached the sliding door slowly, glancing around. The farm was quiet. I searched in the direction of the Swarey's house and my car. It was eerily silent.

A wave of unease stabbed at me and I caught my breath.

The door moved and I froze, raising my gun at the ever-widening gap.

A hand came into view, and then another.

The person's back was to me when he came through the opening. His black knit cap and dungaree coat were typical Amish youth attire.

He turned and his face grew white as a ghost. "Don't shoot!" he begged.

I lowered my weapon. I recognized the kid from the night I found Taylor in the barn. I searched my memories. He was Matthew Troyer. I'd interviewed him at the schoolhouse during the serial killer case. I had immediately pegged him as one of the rowdier kids in the community. The information he'd provided had led me to Charlie Saunders and then back to Monroe in that case.

"Keep your hands up," I ordered.

"It's not us. We didn't kill her," the kid pleaded.

"Shh!" I looked over my shoulder and then back at the boy. His words made my heart begin hammering. "Us? Who are you with?" I whispered.

Matthew swallowed and his gaze darted to the opening. My eyes widened as Daniel's niece stepped out into the snow. Locks of her dark hair were loose from her cap. The bottom of her blue dress was soaked and her boots were muddy. I got a whiff of the awful smell of pigs again and I looked back at the boy. He was covered in muck from his legs down.

"Did you see Monroe or Nicolas?" I asked them.

Sarah spoke up. "We haven't seen Mr. Swarey, but Monroe is around here somewhere."

I pointed at the tracks leading up the hill. "Are those yours?"

The kids nodded.

"Follow them back over the hill and get away from here," I ordered.

Tears dribbled down Sarah's face and it occurred to me how much trouble she was going to get in if she got out of here safely.

"We can't leave Taylor," she said.

A white light exploded in my head. "Taylor's in there?"

"I'm so sorry. It's all my fault—"

I grabbed her shoulder, cutting her babbling off. "Is she all right?"

"She fell in with the pigs and they bit her—and there was a trap door or something—she's stuck in a cellar. Hunter is there with her. We were going for help." She sucked in wet sniffs between words.

I shoved her into Matthew. "Get out of here—now!"

Sarah's mouth dropped open as if she were about to argue with me, but the boy grabbed her arm and tugged her up the hill. I didn't wait to watch them go.

I left the howling wind and snow behind and jumped sideways between the narrow opening. I was back inside the dim barn. I still had my gun drawn as I moved into the shadows. Abandoning any thoughts of sneaking up on either the Swarey father or son, I turned on my light and held it up. There was a stack of hay to one side and that's where I found Hunter Pollard, kneeling on the ground. I covered the distance at a dead run and dropped down beside him.

I shined my flashlight into the hole. "Taylor!" I called down.

There was an unbearable few seconds of silence and then I heard a faint, "Aunt Reni?"

I blinked. "Thank God."

"There's someone down there with her." Hunter's voice was a cold whisper.

The story came together in my mind and I suddenly understood. The truth was more horrifying than my worst fears.

"It's not Pa's fault. She was going to leave us, like a whore in the night."

I whirled around and aimed my gun at Monroe.

His rifle was pointed right back at me. His greasy hair was longish and his face pale. He was short and stout, and just like his dad, his arms were steady with his weapon.

"She wasn't a whore, Monroe. She was an unhappy woman. Becoming Amish didn't suit her well, and you know how your dad treated her." I focused on the teenager's heart. Even if he got a shot off, he would be too dead to hurt Taylor or Hunter. "He was abusive to her, the same as he is to you."

"She drove him to it. If she would have been a better wife and mother, none of this would have happened. If she had kept her husband happy, he wouldn't have gone after either of us. She was going to abandon me to him." Monroe's voice was pitchy, making him sound like a whiny eight-year-old. His hand jerked with emotion and I had the opportunity to take him down. But Monroe's lips trembled and I saw a tear streak down his cheek. My finger froze on the trigger.

He was a troubled kid—a product of his vicious father and resentful mother. It wasn't surprising that he embraced a life of dealing drugs and violence.

"Did you purposely kill Danielle Brown with fentanyl laced heroin?"

His head shook furiously. "The pill head was the one who

talked Ma into leaving. They were going to run away together, with that other woman's help."

"So you punished her?"

He snorted loudly. "She was the one who wanted the stuff. She done killed herself, with Jackson's encouragement. He didn't want her to leave." He shrugged and had a faraway look on his face. "It was God's purpose, I suppose."

Monroe was usually tight-lipped and sullen, but not now. His eyes were wild and his face was wet. The day of reckoning had finally come.

A hundred questions pounded my mind, but Taylor was trapped in a hole, bleeding. And there was someone else down there who needed medical attention as well.

"Put the gun down, Monroe. It's not too late to make everything right. These crimes took place while you were still a minor, a judge will take that into consideration. You can't protect your father anymore. You'll have to tell the truth about what he did." I forced my voice to be gentle, encouraging.

"You mean about the other woman?" His flushed, tear-streaked face smirked. "She's with the pigs—with the pigs." His chest heaved. "She's with the pigs. Oh, the pigs loved the woman." I recognized the look of insanity on the young man's face.

"Drop the gun, Monroe, or I'll shoot you," I ordered.

Monroe sobered and his eyes cleared for a moment. "You don't have to do that, Sheriff. Pa is going to take care of me for you."

A gun blast exploded, and I dropped to the ground beside Hunter. My ears were ringing when I looked up. Monroe lay very still. A dark puddle spread out from his side. He was taking gurgling breaths, and his fingers twitched.

"The boy was touched by evil, just like his mother." Nicolas Swarey appeared from behind the hay. His shotgun was pointed at me. My gun was still in my hand, but it would take a miracle for me to raise it in time to shoot Nicolas before he shot me.

Sweat pooled beneath my jacket and my heart beat like a freight train. My niece was injured in the cellar and another teenager, who'd escaped the school shooting, shook next to me. Daniel might already be dead, too. My head burned with the heat of anger and guilt. I'd been going about my own business for the past few months, while a woman in my jurisdiction was being held captive by her husband. I didn't come for her. It shouldn't have taken another missing woman for me to turn my attention back to Erin Swarey. It was so easy to believe Nicolas Swarey—that his wife had run away. That's what I would have done if I'd been her. But she hadn't gotten away. She'd been here all along. Just like Naomi Beiler—Erin Swarey hadn't made it out of the settlement to freedom.

A ball formed in the pit of my stomach and adrenaline brought my head up.

"But I'm not evil, Nicolas. Neither is this frightened kid beside me or my niece, who fell into that cellar. If you kill us, you're going to be joining your son in hell."

His eyes popped wide and he dipped his head. "None of you should be here. This isn't any of your concern. It's my family, and God gives me authority over my wife and child."

The faint sound of muffled crying from the cellar reached my ears.

"Leave them be, Nick," came a weak voice from the dark hole. "They're innocent. The Lord doesn't want you to take their lives. Just me. I'm the only sinner here. I was too selfish to stay in your world, and I was willing to break my vows to you and abandon my son to get away."

Nicolas stood taller and leered at me. "My wife is wrong about you. You are a sinner, and that's why you're here."

He shifted his weight and I knew he was going to shoot. I ducked and fired my gun, but the sound came a second after another blast rocked the barn. Nicolas hit the ground. His face was a mass of blood and brain matter. Toby returned his revolver to its holster and ran to Monroe's side. He began applying pressure to the wound on the Amish boy's side and lifted his head just briefly enough to wink at me.

Hands gripped me from behind and I breathed in the familiar woodsy scent. Daniel was all right.

I turned in his arms and we rose together. "Help me get down there. Taylor is injured."

Daniel didn't ask any questions. "The ambulance is on the way, along with most of your department."

"He's still alive, Serenity," Toby shouted out.

"Try to keep him that way." I grasped Daniel's arms and he lowered me into the hole.

I stretched out and guessed my feet were a couple of feet from the floor. "Let go," I instructed Daniel.

I dropped, bending my knees to absorb some of the stinging jolt. I turned on my flashlight and found Taylor huddled on the floor with a stranger's arms around her. Dark circles framed the woman's bloodshot, teary eyes. Her brown hair was loose and matted, and I couldn't have guessed what color her dress had originally been. There was a soiled mattress in the corner and several metal pails against the wall. The pungent smell of urine and feces made me hold my breath. When Erin Swarey looked up, I saw bruises on her neck and arms.

As she held my sobbing niece, she muttered, "Is he alive?"

"Your husband is dead, but your son is clinging to life."

"Praise the Lord," she cried. "Thank you."

I knelt in front of Taylor. Her wet eyelashes fluttered. She gasped and lurched at me. I smoothed her damp hair down her back and rocked her tightly against me. Her leg was bloody and her arm was wrapped and limp. But she was alive. She would need a hell of a lot of counseling to get back to some semblance of normalcy again, but at least she would have the opportunity to do just that.

Looking over Taylor's head and into Erin's vacant eyes, I wasn't sure if the woman would ever come back from what had happened to her.

37

SERENITY

"Your mom and dad are waiting at the hospital for you to arrive," I told Taylor. "I have to stay here for little while, but I'll be in town to visit you as soon as I can. Daniel is going to ride in the ambulance with you. Are you okay with that?"

She managed a wavering smile at Daniel and then looked back at me. "Yeah, I'll be fine. After all, he's practically part of the family, right?" Her smile became coy and I caught a glimpse of my mischievous niece.

"In two weeks, we make it official," I said.

"Thanks for saving me again, Aunt Reni."

"You better not make this a habit," I teased, squeezing her hand. "Beth and Raymond will take good care of you."

I stepped back and let the EMTs lift the gurney into the ambulance.

"We've got her, Serenity. No worries," Beth said as she worked.

"I know, you've got this." I turned to Daniel. Before I could

EVIL IN MY TOWN

say anything, he leaned into me and kissed my lips. I swayed a little and his hand steadied me.

"I'll see you later," he whispered into my ear.

The thought of sometime later that night, climbing under the covers to his warmth caused the side of my mouth to rise. "Yes, you will."

Watching the ambulance drive away, I had mixed emotions. Relief flooded me that Taylor was going to be all right, and the other was deep annoyance that I couldn't go with her. But I had a job to do.

The blinking lights turned on and the siren wailed. One of the buggy horses pranced in place and the other whinnied when the ambulance drove by. I didn't feel the usual prickling sensation in my gut when the bishop approached. We didn't always see eye to eye, but he was on my side this time.

The man at his side was an older version of Daniel, and he was frowning deeply. Moses was always grumpy, but his strong features were even more stark than usual. I assumed he had come to retrieve his granddaughter. She was standing between Hunter and the Amish boy. Bobby was talking to them. The kids had stumbled down the hillside when the first patrol cars arrived.

I shook my head. They were a couple of seriously rebellious kids. Aaron and Moses were going to have their work cut out for them.

Blue and red lights flashed against the white blanket of snow. The snowfall had tapered off and the wind had died down to a stiff, cold breeze.

I glanced over my shoulder at the other ambulance. The EMTs were hovering over Monroe. He was already hooked up to an oxygen bag. His eyes were closed and a blanket covered his bloody body. Erin Swarey held his hand. Her face was smudged with dirt and tears. Her hair was a tangled mess. Dark purple bruises covered her cheeks, and there was a crimson line around her neck. I assumed her husband had routinely beaten her and even attempted to strangle her, but I'd have to wait for the details when I formally interviewed the woman the following day. Although she didn't seem to have any broken bones or life-threatening injuries, she was dangerously thin. She would get a thorough examination and counseling at the hospital. The timing of my talk with her would also depend on if her son survived. She stared with emotionless, dead eyes at Monroe, and I feared she might not be able to give a clear picture of what she'd actually been through, or the fate of her friend, Charlene.

"Looks like you solved another one, Sheriff."

I raised my brows at Toby as he walked up. An amused grin was fixated on his mouth. His eyes were light and dancing.

"This one was just blind luck. I never expected Erin Swarey to be alive and locked up in a cellar in a barn. I'm just happy we got here in time to save my niece and the other kids. Who knows what Nicolas or Monroe would have done to them once their secret was discovered."

"There's a good chance it would have turned ugly." He tilted his head and looked at me from under his hat. "You followed your gut and some solid leads. It wasn't mere chance we arrived in time. I call it focused persistence."

"I appreciate all your help—on the case and back there," I thumbed over my shoulder toward the barn.

He shrugged and looked away. "It's my job." He pulled out his phone and flashed the screen. There were several messages from John Ruthers, his boss. "It looks like my day job is in need of my services. I'll head back to your office with Todd and write up an official report about what transpired here, and then I'll be on my way."

I hesitated and touched his arm. "If you ever need my help, you know where to find me. I owe you one."

He tipped his hat and his crooked grin returned. "Oh, I got your number, Sheriff. I might just take you up on your offer one day." He turned and then pivoted back. "Congratulations on your upcoming wedding. Daniel is good guy. You'll be happy."

He was walking away before I could respond. It was probably better I didn't say anything. There was just enough chemistry between me and the lawman to make discussing my upcoming marriage uncomfortable. But it was nice to have a person like him to call if I was ever in a bind.

"Serenity, may I speak with you?" Bobby waddled through the snow. Snowflakes clung to his grey mustache and his round cheeks were red from the cold. Hunter was with him.

"Sure. Did you get a look at the hog pen?" I asked.

He nodded briskly. "I did. The pigs will have to be moved somewhere else so we can search the pen for any more of Charlene Noble's remains."

"Any more?" I looked between Bobby and Hunter. "You found something?" That was news to me.

Bobby gestured at the bag Hunter held tightly in his hands. It had a picture of a pig on it and read *FEED*. "It's going to take some stripping that pen down and searching through the manure and mud. I don't expect we'll find much, but this"— he nodded at the bag—"should be enough to close the case on Charlene's disappearance."

"They fed her to the pigs?" My stomach tightened.

"Certainly looks that way. Hopefully, Mrs. Swarey can shed light on how her friend ended up in the pen, or if Monroe survives, we might get more information from him."

Hunter held out the bag to me and I took it. "Thanks for being there for Taylor. Go on home and get some sleep. I want you and your folks to come into the department first thing in the morning."

"I already told your deputy everything and he wrote it all down."

"Yes, well, I have a lot more questions for you. This case is going to be a paper nightmare. So, I'll see you in the morning?"

He nodded. "Yeah, I'll be there." He paused. "Is it okay if I stop by the hospital tonight before I go home? I'd like to see Taylor."

I narrowed my eyes on the young man. He was taller than me and muscled more than the average teenager. He had blond hair and blue eyes. I could see why Taylor might find him attractive, but none of that mattered to me. The kid had stayed with my niece when most would have fled the scene. He was also with her the day of the school shooting, making him fairly dependable and all right in my book.

"I don't have a problem with it." I smiled politely. "It's her parents you're going to have to win over. If you think I'm tough, just wait until you meet my sister."

Hunter swallowed and nodded, backing away.

"That wasn't very nice," Bobby said.

I shot him a withering look. "After this week, let me have my fun." I opened the bag and the smell of pig shit assailed my senses. I flashed my light into the bag and quickly looked up. "Is that her foot?"

"It sure is. Taylor grabbed hold of it when she fell in with the pigs." Bobby jerked a little and I figured he had experienced the same shuddering jolt I had thinking about how my niece might have ended up in the same way poor Charlene Noble had. "You know, in the not so distance past, pigs were the usual mode of disposal for murder victims. As recently as 2002, Robert Pickton, a pig farmer in Canada, was arrested for the murders of dozens of women. He fed them to the pigs, whether they were alive or already dead when they met their fate, is anyone's guess."

I held up my hand to stop Bobby from talking and rolled the top of the bag down. I shoved the bag into his hands. The coroner's fascination with death would have startled most people, but I was used to it. With the scent of the pig manure on the breeze, and a woman's foot in the bag, the bile rose into my throat.

"Enough talk about pigs for now. Please." I shook the image from my mind. "I asked Todd to call Charlene's sister and tell her that we believe we have Charlene's remains. I want you to make it a priority to get the DNA back so we can give the family closure as soon as possible."

"I'll start on it tonight. I'll work on Nicolas Swarey in the morning."

I watched the old man plod to his car, carrying the bag. I shook my head. What an awful way to go.

"Are you cold, Sheriff?"

Aaron Esch had snuck up on me. I ignored his question. Moses led Sarah and Matthew to his buggy. My future father-in-law glanced my way, but kept walking. Sarah raised her hand, and I returned the gesture.

As if the bishop had read my mind, he said, "You're welcome to talk to the children tomorrow afternoon. The elders will want to speak with them in the morning."

I was relieved he was giving me access to them the

following day. I contemplated his slender, foxlike face. The Amish leader could be a real pain in my ass on some days, but today his expression was thoughtful.

"Nicolas Swarey is dead. He had a shotgun pointed at me and was ready to fire. The US Marshal shot him in the head. He died instantly." He nodded slowly, absorbing my words. "All this time, Erin Swarey was being held in the barn cellar, against her will. She was starved and beaten. It appears that Nicolas found out about his wife's plan to leave him. Monroe knew where she was all along. I'm not sure yet how much he actually had to do with her captivity, but he admitted to knowing she was down there. Erin had a friend who tried to help her get away, and that woman ended up in the pig pen. You can guess what happened to her."

The bishop cringed and his eyes darted away. He stared at the second ambulance when it turned onto the roadway. The sound of its sirens wailed over the countryside. A patrol car pulled out behind it, following it into the night.

When the sirens faded, he asked, "Will Monroe live?"

"I don't know." I met the bishop's gaze. "Nicolas shot him in the stomach. He's in bad shape, but it could go either way."

"It would be better if that boy joined his father."

His words stunned me. I closed my mouth and stood still. "That's pretty harsh. I'm surprised you'd say something like that. I thought you always forgave." I remembered back to how the Amish in the Strasburg community in Pennsylvania had forgiven the man who had shot up the Coblenz wedding. At the time, their reluctance to hold a grudge had bothered me immensely. But hearing a man of God wish a young man dead from his own community was even worse.

The bishop pressed his lips together and offered me a patient look. "In this case, it's not about forgiveness. The well-being of my people is the utmost importance. We must preserve our way of life. Monroe was a cancer to our other children. There was no counselling, punishment, or change of circumstance that would have kept him from the evil gripping his heart." He looked at me with flat eyes. "If he lives, others will suffer, in time."

He was right. Monroe was completely fucked up. There was no way to undo the dysfunction he'd experienced leading up to the day his dad shot him. I wasn't convinced that he hadn't purposely sold Danielle tainted heroin with the hopes of killing her. Jackson's corpse lying on the table in the examination room at the mortuary appeared in my mind. The teenagers were very similar. They had both come from troubled home lives, and they didn't fit in anywhere. Would Monroe become a cold-blooded killer, like Jackson, if he recovered? Only time would tell.

"It's in God's hands now," I said.

The bishop's eyes widened. "I'm glad you understand that, Sheriff. It gives me hope for you."

I rolled my eyes and left the holy man. A team was gathered in front of the barn to begin taking and recording evidence. It was dark and freezing, but my work was just beginning.

I was exhausted and would need coffee soon. Twenty-eight people. Dead. Twenty-seven at the school earlier in the week, and Nicolas Swarey tonight. Monroe might add to that count by morning. Then there were Charlene Noble and Danielle Brown, and before them were Makayla Bowman and Hannah Kuhns. Add Eli Bender and Ada Mae to the list. And of course, Naomi Beiler. The body count in Blood Rock always seemed to be rising.

The bishop was right. There was evil in my town.

38

SERENITY

December 19th

I stared at my reflection in the mirror. They had done a pretty good job at the hair salon. My blonde locks were swept up into a relaxed bun. Several wisps framed my face, and small lavender colored flowers were positioned just right in a few spots in my hair. I loved the contrast of the pop of color with the white dress. CJ had just finished painting my face, and I thought I resembled a china doll. By the fawning look on her freckled face, she was pleased with her work.

CJ drew back. "You're gorgeous, Serenity."

"As much time was put into transforming me, I would hope I look pretty good." I grinned until I saw the slight frown develop on her face. I lowered my voice. "Is everything all right?"

She quickly forced a wide smile. "Oh, yes. Don't mind me. It's nothing."

I released the deep breath I'd been holding in. The entire morning was nothing but a blur of running around and primping. I looked forward to climbing into bed with Daniel that night, and heading off to the sand and palm trees in the morning. The ceremony part was giving me fits. I didn't understand why most women wanted all the pomp and pageantry of a formal wedding ceremony. I would have been just fine tying the knot at the courthouse, with a few important people present. This torturous day was because of Daniel. He was the one who wanted something special and meaningful. To me, the first few hours were nothing compared to the rest of our lives—now that was going to be where the real marriage began.

The only reason I'd made it this far was because of CJ. She had held my hand the past two weeks. Every time I came seriously close to backing out, she was there, encouraging and cajoling me to this point in time, where I was only minutes away from walking down the aisle and becoming Daniel's wife.

"Is it Joshua?" I asked in a soft voice.

CJ shrugged, looked away and back again. Her green eyes glistened. "I think I made a mistake. I'm miserable without him."

I took her hands and squeezed. I hated getting married while my friend's own love life was a mess. The worst part about it was that there wasn't anything I could do for her. "It's an impossible situation. You probably did the right thing."

She nodded vigorously, sucking in a wispy breath. "Oh, I know, but it still hurts like hell. I love him, Serenity. But I have to let him go—he's Amish, and I'm not." She straightened up and dabbed her eyes. "It's your wedding day. I will not be sad." Her gaze strayed to the window. Powdery flakes gently fell and the street lamps illuminated the fresh snow that had blanketed the town the night before. "It's just plain wrong for me to be worrying about my love life when all those kids died..."

Her voice trailed off into silence and a cold chill fluttered across my skin. I had stared down murderers and barely broken a sweat. Now I was melting under the tension of making a lifelong commitment to another person. My near panic attack was even more ridiculous by the events earlier in the month. Dozens of innocent young people and several teachers had lost their lives in a school shooting in my town. It was a disgusting act of violence that most people only witness from afar, on their newsfeed or cable television. Something I didn't think would ever happen in my own backyard, had happened. And no one in our community was unscathed by the mindless killings. Jackson Merritt's troubled life had led to a life of horror for countless others.

While I stood in the small room at the back of the remodeled antebellum building, with the large oval mirror and my friend CJ, I couldn't shake the question of *why*—why did some people snap and go off the rails, while the rest of us dealt with our problems, depression, or anxiety? Why did Jackson Merritt really do it? Could he have been stopped before he snapped, or was it an event that the freedoms we hold dear in our country made inevitable? There were no good answers to these questions, at least not right now. Perhaps in time we'd figure it all out, but I feared that at the base of it all was the reality that evil did exist. And that wickedness was here to stay.

My thoughts lingered to the curse that was supposedly laid on our town two hundred years earlier when outlaws butchered a Native American family down by the river, and a church congregation on the hill overlooking Blood Rock. I wasn't usually a superstitious person, but in the past year, I'd witnessed acts that made me begin to question my own belief system. Everything wasn't always black and white, good or evil. A hell of a lot of things couldn't be explained away by science or rational thinking, like what had happened at the Swarey farm. A family was completely destroyed—the father dead and the mother's mind nearly broken. Monroe had survived the gunshot wound to his stomach, but he had a long road to recovery ahead of him, and a jail cell waiting for him when he was released from the hospital. Monroe's admissions about Danielle Brown had led to several other fentanyl overdoses, and his drug supplier. He was implicated in those deaths, along with conspiracy to kidnapping charges regarding his mother.

Erin Swarey had insisted that her husband had accidently killed her friend, Charlene Noble, in a fit of rage. When he caught the woman in his home, helping his wife escape her life with him, he'd shoved the woman and she had fallen, striking her head on the corner of a chest. The forensic tests had proven that the red smudge on the chest was in fact, Charlene's blood. If Erin's story was true, it meant her poor friend was at least dead when she was thrown in with the pigs.

"Stop it!" CJ took my hands and tugged me to the door. "Let go of the awful memories. It's time to get married."

The knock at the door yanked me from my dark thoughts. CJ looked at me and I nodded. She cracked the door open to see who it was. My sister came in, with Taylor in tow.

"Oh my, gosh, Serenity. You look beautiful." Laura gave me a quick hug. "I wish Mom and Dad were here to see you walk down the aisle."

Dad and Mom had been gone for five years. Dad had died from complications following heart surgery, and feisty Mom had passed away later that same year after a long battle with cancer. The second half of their lives had been plagued by illness, but they'd still made it to forty happy years together.

It pinched my heart that they weren't here to share this day with us, and I'd always feel bad that Daniel didn't get to meet them. But I knew them, and they'd want me to embrace happiness and not shed any tears on their account. I'd already done that enough years ago. Laura, as the oldest sister, had stepped in to take their places. I rarely thought of them anymore. Occasionally, some milestone would occur that made them suddenly appear in my mind. This was one those occasions. I worked hard to keep from crying when I looked at my sister. "Dad would have laughed, and Mom would have said something inappropriate."

I grinned and she chuckled.

"Yep. That's how they would have reacted," Laura said.

"Is your husband here?" I asked carefully, watching the expression on my sister's face go from a smile to an even deeper one.

She nodded. "With everything that Taylor went through," she glanced at her daughter "we've decided to make our marriage work. We have so many blessings. Our problems seem trivial now."

This time, I couldn't keep the tears from pooling in my eyes. I threw my arms around Laura and Taylor. "I'm so happy to hear it. That's wonderful news."

"Thanks for being there for Taylor when she needed you most," Laura whispered in my ear.

I tussled Taylor's hair. She jumped back, trying to protect the fancy curls that the hairdresser had created for the wedding. "That's what aunts are supposed to do, right?"

"Maybe if they're also the town's sheriff," Taylor said, smirking.

She looked so different than when we pulled her out of

that murky hole in the barn. Her cheeks were rosy and her eyes bright. The long-sleeved purple dress she wore covered the bandage on her arm and the hemline was just long enough to cover the sutures from the bite on her leg. Taylor's frame of mind was improving every day. Kids were resilient and I hoped that my niece could truly move past the terrors that she had experienced.

CJ handed me a tissue and forced me to stand still while she brushed some makeup below my eyes and over my cheeks. "No more emotions! Your face will not hold up if you begin crying."

I raised my hands, fending her off. "I'm fine." I glanced at the clock on the wall. "Why don't we get this over with," I suggested.

"Are you ready?" Laura asked.

"As ready as I'm ever going to be."

CJ handed Taylor and Laura their bouquets and lined them up. She peeked out the door. "It's time," she breathed.

The music drifted in through the doorway. I stared down at the white and purple flowers in my hands. My legs turned to jelly and I swayed a bit.

This was it. It was really happening.

39

SERENITY

Will winked and I smiled back. My nephew was eight inches taller than me, but I still remembered when he used to snuggle up beside me on the couch and I'd read the Harry Potter books to him. He had flown from Montana back to Blood Rock the day before, and he hadn't come alone. The girl he'd introduced was an equestrian like him. She was friendly and down to earth. I was glad that he'd found someone special and that he had moved on from his tragic relationship with the Amish girl, Naomi Beiler.

He took his sister's arm and they led the procession up the aisle way that had been created between the white folding chairs. A garland of pine, peppered with purple flowers, connected the chairs. In front of the large room was a fireplace. It had an ornate wooden mantel piece. A happy fire danced in the logs, warming the high-ceilinged room. More garland rested across the hearth and flowers decorated the place where Daniel and I would stand.

Daniel was there, waiting for me. I spied on him from

the gap in the doorway. He stood tall and proud in front of the guests. His thick, dark hair was brushed neatly, and he'd trimmed his jawline just enough to still have a sexy shading of stubble, like I'd requested. He looked more comfortable in his purple tie and black suit than I felt in my long dress. A smile fluttered on his lips and I wondered if he could have possibly seen me spying on him from across the room.

Todd saluted me before he joined CJ and they followed my niece and nephew up the aisle. He wore his usual smirk, and when his head dipped down to say something into CJ's ear, she shook with laughter. I imagined he'd said something sarcastic about the fact that I was actually getting married. Out of all of my friends, he'd been the most supportive and contradicting. One minute he was praising my decision, and the next he was saying prayers for Daniel. Todd had been annoying me since we were kids. I was sure nothing would change after I was married.

Since all of Daniel's closest friends and family were Amish, they hadn't been allowed to attend the wedding, let alone serve as a best man. So, Daniel chose his future brother-in-law for the part. It seemed fitting that my sister had the opportunity to walk down the aisle with her husband once again. And at the time we'd made plans, we'd hoped it might rekindle the spark in their marriage. It seemed to have worked. They smiled at each other when they locked arms.

My stomach rolled in waves when I stepped through the doorway. I found Bobby standing to the side, waiting for me. He looked very dapper in his purple vest and black suit. He dipped his gray head in a curt nod and offered his arm.

The music sounded far away. Bobby mumbled something about my dress, but I didn't understand him. Our steps were slow, similar to walking through deep snow. I concentrated on lifted my feet and putting them back down. Familiar faces popped up everywhere in the sea of people. The mayor waved and Elayne Weaver smiled brightly. Heather, Todd's wife, was trying to quiet their baby, but she glanced up in time to see me walk by. She gave me a thumbs up. Deputy Jeremy Dickens, and Rosie, the receptionist, sat together. Nancy leaned out over the garland to touch my arm when I came close.

"I am so jealous." Nancy smacked her lips and winked.

The slinky look on her face loosened me up. I couldn't help smirking back at the older woman.

The walk seemed to take forever, but when I reached the preacher, it wasn't nearly long enough. Bobby released me and I took the last two steps by myself to stop in front of the podium, beside Daniel. His hand enclosed around mine and he grinned at me. There was a twinkle in his eyes that promised kisses in the dark. I loved that look. It made my knees weak, but in a good way. When the butterflies exploded in my belly, I asked myself again, how did I get so lucky? I didn't deserve this handsome and gentle man looking down at me. We'd sure had our ups and downs, but I was so thankful he'd picked me. I never would have survived the murder and mayhem of the past year without him. My eyes passed over his muscled shoulders and his set jawline and I knew he'd be my rock for future criminal investigations. Not to mention life in general.

I reluctantly tore my eyes from my almost husband to stare at the pastor. Daniel had insisted that we were married by a man of God. I agreed on the condition that I wouldn't have to join a church or commit myself to weekly Sunday services. The only thing this particular preacher requested was that Daniel and I meet with him one time to discuss the wedding and our future life together. We did just that a few days earlier, and our discussion had gone from the usual man and wife mumbo jumbo to my job and the recent horrific events in Blood Rock. The pastor's wisdom had given me hope that even though evil walked among us, so did many good people. And that I wasn't alone in my battle to save people from that evil. The meeting with the pastor reminded me of the many occasions when the bishop or other people in the Amish community had talked about faith and what it actually meant. When my eyes met the pastor's, he smiled reassuringly, and I let out a slow breath. He hadn't judged me, and I was happy for that.

A disturbance at the back of the room turned all of our heads. Cold air blew in from the entryway as the doors pushed open. I couldn't believe my eyes. A crowd of dark cloaked people emerged from the snowy exterior.

Daniel stiffened beside me and I glanced up. His eyes were watering and his lips trembled slightly. He gripped my hand tighter and his mouth spread into a wide smile.

Bishop Aaron Esch led the way to the only empty row of seats. Moses and Anna Bachman were right behind him. Daniel's sister Rebecca lifted her hand and I waved back. She nudged her husband forward. Sarah, Christina, and the rest of the Daniel's nieces and nephews lined up against the back wall. I caught Taylor and Sarah exchange silent words. It seemed their friendship was the real deal. It would forever be tested because of their different cultures, but it might survive in the end. Lester Lapp and his crazy wife, Ester, came through the doorway next, along with their son Mervin and his girlfriend, Verna. Katherine's doll-like face was smiling as she stepped up beside her husband, Joseph.

"I thought they weren't coming," I whispered.

"Me too," Daniel replied. He was beaming.

The last through the doorway were Joshua Miller, his three children, and his elderly grandmother, Nana. I leaned forward to see CJ. The color had drained from her face.

Joshua's gaze found CJ immediately and my heart stuttered at the intensity of his stare in her direction. CJ might try to move on and forget about the Amish man, but something in the way he looked at her made me think that he wasn't going to allow that to happen.

Once the newcomers had taken their seats or found a space along the wall to stand, the room finally quieted.

"You may carry on," the bishop said loudly from the back of the room.

The crowd erupted in laughter as Daniel and I turned back to the preacher.

Our ceremony was not very long. The pastor said a Bible verse and a prayer. He spoke for a few minutes about marriage and love. When it came time to exchange our vows, everything that the preacher had just said was a blur. Daniel had explained to me that Amish weddings were three-hour long affairs, sitting on hard benches, and remaining silent except for a few stoic hymns. The main event was the dinner that was usually roasted chicken, with all the trimmings. He had told me that the bride didn't wear a white dress and the couple didn't exchange rings. I wondered what the Amish people thought about our wedding, and how Daniel really felt about it. Did a part of him miss being Amish? It was a question that had haunted our relationship from the beginning, and still gave me pause today.

Daniel tugged on my hand and I turned to him. Will

stepped forward and handed Daniel the rings. He offered me an encouraging nod before stepping back to his place with Taylor.

The cool metal of the ring slipping onto my finger woke me from the cloudy haze.

"I promise to love you in good times and in bad—completely and forever," Daniel said.

I swallowed the knot down in my throat. My heart beat wildly and I felt a little dizzy. But Daniel's gaze was steady and reassuring. He looked confident, and that confidence gave me the strength to put the ring onto his hand and repeat the vows.

"I now pronounce you man and wife"—the pastor paused for effect—"you may kiss your bride."

"Ah, the best part," Daniel said.

He bent down and my lips parted. Whoops and hollers followed, and a thundering applause. Our kiss deepened and the music began. For a moment I was lost in the kiss. Daniel's arms were around me and his tongue was in my mouth. Everyone else disappeared, and so did the melancholy and bad memories of the past. It was a new beginning. I would embrace it with everything I had. After all, I knew more than most people how fleeting life was. Happiness was a miracle I wouldn't take for granted.

Daniel's mouth pulled away. "I love you, Serenity."

"I love you, too."

40

SERENITY

It took a while to work my way around to the Amish contingent. The caterers handed out champagne glasses and Swedish meatballs on tiny plates. There was a cacophony of sounds, from the DJ's playlist to the guests mingling. Todd was one of the louder voices in the crowd. He was showing off his baby girl and joking around with Nancy about how he was going to ward off any possible suitors for the girl's attention when she was a teenager.

Daniel had finally separated from me and was enjoying a slap on the back from his best childhood friend, Lester. Joseph and his dad, Moses, were offering him sage advice on being a good husband. Most of which, they admitted, probably went out the window when you're married to the sheriff.

Rebecca and Laura were striking up a conversation while their daughters huddled in the corner, whispering to each other. Seeing the two very different women laughing together raised my spirits even more. Maybe there was hope for Taylor and Sarah after all.

Daniel's mother was a petite woman, but the strength of her hug surprised me. "I pray your household will be blessed with children," she said. Anna wasn't shy about her desire for even more grandkids.

I forced a tight smile. "We're discussing it." I leaned in. "Trust me, you'll be one of the first to know when it happens."

My choice of words seemed to please her immensely. She smiled from ear to ear.

"How did you pull this off?" I motioned to the other Amish around the room.

"There are rules we live by and abide, but sometimes things come up that don't fit into the mold. This was one of those times. Katherine, Rebecca, and I went before the elders and argued the case for us to come and honor your wedding to Daniel. In years past, nothing we said would have changed the men's minds, but the events of the last year have changed us all. Without your help and guidance, who knows where we would be. Your actions have saved our children on several occasions. We convinced the bishop and ministers that the respect we hold for you outweighs the act of shunning Daniel." She tilted her head and leaned in closer, lowering her voice. "It wasn't very hard to convince the bishop. He wanted to attend."

"Thank you for going to bat for us. It means a lot to Daniel—and to me."

"I know, dear. You must stop by next week. I have a quilt I made for the two of you. It's nearly finished, and there's several quarts of canned soup for your cupboards."

Anna was now officially my mother-in-law. My heart fluttered at the thought. But the idea of her homemade soup made my stomach rumble. For all of our cultural differences and their annoying restrictions, one thing I never had a problem with was Amish food.

Anna left me to join a cluster of women that included CJ, Katherine, Heather, Esther, and Nana. I wondered what they would talk about when my gaze settled on Joshua. He stood close enough to the group conversing with Daniel to be included with them, but his eyes kept drifting back to CJ. I caught her glancing up, meeting his gaze, and looking away.

A sense of foreboding raced through me, making me clench my hands.

"Nothing good will come from that, I can tell you."

The bishop had snuck up on me. He was looking in the same direction as I, and I had no doubt he was talking about CJ and Joshua.

"Perhaps I'm wrong. She's different than Erin Swarey. The young woman might make a fine Amish woman," the bishop said. His brow rose when he looked at me.

"That isn't going to happen," I said confidently, but my gaze drifted back to CJ. Was love really that blind?

"Stranger things have happened. You know that better than most." He raised his head and surveyed the room. "It's good to see our people mingling and at peace. A celebration is just what was needed to lighten everyone's hearts."

I sighed. "It's been a rough year. I hope we get a long run of boredom around here. I think we're due, don't you?"

When I looked back at the bishop, he was staring at me. His features were rigid and his eyes shadowed. Goosebumps rose on my arms.

"We are forever tested in this world of evil." His attention sharpened. "We are God's soldiers, you and I. It is our duty to always be ready for the onslaught. I fear another battle is just around the corner."

Dammit. It was my wedding day. The crusty old Amish leader was not going to freak me out and ruin my day.

I couldn't stop myself from asking, "What the hell are you talking about?"

"Do you remember our friends in the Poplar Springs settlement?"

My mind whirled. Was this conversation really happening? I remembered when the bishop showed up at my office with Rowan Schwartz last winter. There had been a rash of barn burnings in the northern community. They were looking for someone who understood the rules and laws of the outside world, but also respected the Amish culture and its differences. I had been intrigued and reluctantly headed north to investigate. Daniel had helped on the case and it was there, at Rowan's farm, that we'd finally succumbed to our attraction for each other. What I had discovered there, turned out to be seedy underground crime world, connected to the Amish that had nearly gotten me killed.

I drew in a deep breath, forcing my voice to remain steady. "Of course I remember. It would be impossible to forget something like that."

He nodded slowly. "Rowan may be in need of our help again. If I call on you in the future, will you be available? Discretion is important in this matter."

I felt as if I was in a mafia movie, and the bishop was the head don, pulling the puppet strings and asking for favors. A shiver swept through me, but I liked Rowan and his children. Anna was a good woman. If I had the opportunity to help them, could I possibly turn the bishop down?

Daniel caught my eye from across the room. He mouthed, *I love you.* A deep sense of regret filled me. I would forever bring chaos into his life. It would never end.

As much as I detested it starting all over again, I couldn't deny the intense curiosity that had suddenly sharpened my senses.

No, it wouldn't end—and I couldn't stop being me. Daniel knew what he was getting himself into when he stuck that ring on my finger.

I finally met the bishop's intense gaze. "That's why you came to the wedding, huh?"

He shrugged. "It made the women happy, and I was hoping you'd appreciate the gesture."

"Cut the bullshit. You don't have to manipulate me to get your way. I'll do whatever I can to help Rowan and his family, and you know it."

"I'm not a betting man, Sheriff. It's always best to have a backup plan, don't you think?"

I reached out and snatched a glass of champagne off the waiter's tray and took a large gulp. "Oh, yeah, I know all about backup plans."

Look for Forbidden Ways, the romantic companion novel to Serenity's Plain Secrets, to come out in 2019, and the next chapter in Serenity's story to hit the shelves in 2020

Thank you for reading!

You can find Karen Ann Hopkins and all her books at https://www.karenannhopkins.com

Made in the USA
San Bernardino, CA
16 July 2019